THE DANCE

The music was insidiously romantic, and the chandeliers appeared to spin above as Alastair whirled Cressida around, ever faster, dipping and swaying. She was exquisitely aware of his closeness, of the intimate warmth of his hand through the silk of her gown. Was it of her he thought, or Alice?

The music swept to a triumphant close—and with it returned a measure of sanity. "You dance well," he said, releasing her rather too abruptly.

"I had an accomplished partner," she said lightly, and hoped he would not detect the fast beating of her heart.

Lady Kilbride, watching them from her place on the little dais with Lady Sefton, felt her heart quicken a little. If only . . . surely there was more than the usual partiality between these two young people who meant so much to her? That would fulfill all her dreams. . . .

The Lady
from Lisbon

Sheila Walsh

A SIGNET BOOK

SIGNET
Published by New American Library, a division of
Penguin Putnam Inc., 375 Hudson Street,
New York, New York 10014, U.S.A.
Penguin Books Ltd, 27 Wrights Lane,
London W8 5TZ, England
Penguin Books Australia Ltd, Ringwood,
Victoria, Australia
Penguin Books Canada Ltd, 10 Alcorn Avenue,
Toronto, Ontario, Canada M4V 3B2
Penguin Books (N.Z.) Ltd, 182–190 Wairau Road,
Auckland 10, New Zealand

Penguin Books Ltd, Registered Offices:
Harmondsworth, Middlesex, England

First published by Signet, an imprint of New American Library,
a division of Penguin Putnam Inc.

First Printing, February 2001
10 9 8 7 6 5 4 3 2 1

PUBLISHER'S NOTE
This is a work of fiction. Names, characters, places, and incidents either
are the product of the author's imagination or are used fictitiously,
and any resemblance to actual persons, living or dead, business establish-
ments, events, or locales is entirely coincidental.

Chapter One

" **A** nd so, my dear Alastair, I immediately thought of you . . ."

"You are too kind, Aunt Beatrice," murmured the sixth earl of Langley, his mind almost wholly absorbed in contemplation of the evening ahead. Lady Milchester's soirees were invariably graced by the cream of society, among whom society's latest darling, Isabella Devine, outshone all others. Her liaisons were always discreet and she could choose from any number of willing suitors. He alone had declined to worship at her shrine, well aware that his apparent indifference piqued her. He meant to have her, of course, in the fullness of time, but it would be on his terms.

His aunt's voice intruded once more.

"Kindness don't come into it, m'boy. You are my nearest kin, and the matter is a delicate one—a family matter, in fact."

"Nothing that can't be sorted out, I daresay," he murmured. "As ever, you know I am yours to command."

"Why, so I had hoped. It concerns my goddaughter, and perhaps more pertinently, her father. The plain fact is, if he were not my late husband's dearest friend, I would think very ill of Charles Merriton—very ill indeed—for what father with any paternal feeling would leave his only child to the care of others to face what must still be deemed a dangerous journey to England by sea while he goes galloping off to

France at Lord Wellington's behest—and all at a moment's notice?"

The earl sighed, relinquishing for the present a tantalizing memory of cerulean blue eyes that teased and promised much, of gold-tipped lashes, thick and curling, a body as supple as a wand . . . and gave attention once more to his plump, prosaic aunt, who was in many ways very like this room in which she spent most of her days—a room overflowing with heavy furniture and depressing draperies, and knickknacks on every conceivable surface. He could remember a time, before the death of his uncle, when things had been quite different—when Aunt Beatrice had been full of life—at the very hub of every fashionable ball or gathering of note. Now, though of no great age, she had apparently lost all interest in life and seldom left the house, so that only a few of her most devoted friends ever paid her a visit. And he sometimes wondered whether the poor apology for a companion she employed did not depress her even further.

"Well, Alastair?" He collected his thoughts to consider her question.

"One with a restless spirit and willing friends, perhaps," he hazarded. "Also a gift for diplomacy, allied to a positive genius for wriggling out of impossible situations equal only to Lord Wellington's, which Merriton has done more times than enough."

"None of which excuses his present conduct."

"Perhaps not. But the way I heard it, it was Wellington—or Wellesley as he then was—who persuaded Merriton to accompany him when he first set out—oh, it must be all of six years ago—for Portugal with his troops—told him that having a man of his fine negotiating skills on hand in Lisbon could be invaluable when victory came. How is that for optimism—to be that sure when all seems to be against you? They are two of a kind in many ways, I'd say. It has all taken rather longer than expected, but now, with this interminable war coming to an end at last, and Wellington close to Paris, Merriton's diplomatic skills will be given full rein."

"Stuff and nonsense. Oh, it is true that Wellington esteems Charles highly, but it is equally possible that he is grown bored with life in Lisbon. It wouldn't be the first time."

Her nephew quirked an eyebrow. There was a sharpness in her voice whenever Merriton's name was mentioned, and he had a vague recollection that, years ago, there had been something between them, though it would not do to mention it.

"Well, you know him a great deal better than I, so I would not presume to dispute your reasoning, Aunt Bea. Men like Charles Merriton and Wellington are at their best when faced with a challenge. Nor would I dispute that especially if it is to be found in congenial surroundings. Lisbon must have long since palled, and where better than Paris—even a Paris reduced to a state of turmoil by war—to discover many new and delightful distractions to engage his interest."

Lady Kilbride bit back the temptation to accuse him of displaying unwarranted levity. For in truth, Alastair had changed out of all recognition since his disastrous liaison with that wretched Lady Alice Waring—a prodigious beauty who had all but thrown herself at him, only to abandon him in favor of Viscount Sherbourne, who was more than twice her age and ugly as sin, but whose fortune was legendary. Within a twelvemonth, Sherbourne was dead, and she an extremely wealthy woman. It was rumored she had fled to Vienna, largely to escape the two-year tedium of widowhood—and most probably in the hope that her money would attract a congenial lover. It must be all of four years since, but her cruelty must have hurt Alastair more than he would ever let on, for it had bred in him a cynicism that he still wore like a protective shell. He had also, if rumor was to be believed, acquired a repu-

tation which she privately deplored, of having become
something of a libertine.

Watching him now, apparently at ease, sprawled in
her late husband's chair, with one long, elegantly pan-
talooned leg crossed over the other, his dark hair
cropped and swirling in one of the latest fashions, and
his chin sunk in a cravat, the folds of which she had
heard those who knew about such nonsensical matters,
say to be of a deceptive simplicity that rivalled Brummell
at his peak, one might be forgiven for thinking him a
frippery fellow until one looked into those dark, enigmatic eyes. Then, one could almost believe the other
thing that was said of him—that he was a dangerous
man to cross. Only his continuing care of her, and the
occasional glimpse of the charming youth he had once
been, gave hope that he was not beyond redemption.

"As I recall, Merriton took his family to Lisbon
with him."

Lady Kilbride uttered a most unladylike grunt.
"Which was a wicked thing to do in my opinion. I
cannot imagine how Wellesley could have allowed a
mother and child on a ship filled with rough soldiers,
and danger lurking wherever one might turn, for at that
time Napoleon was set upon conquering all before
him. Any man of sense would have put his foot down.
But then, charming fellow though I'll allow Charles to
be, with many qualities to commend him, I long ago
concluded that Arabella could twist him 'round her
little finger anytime she chose to do so—Wellesley,
too, I shouldn't wonder. They say he also has an eye
for a pretty woman."

There was an unaccustomed note of venom in this
condemnation that again brought to mind rumors he
had overheard as a boy, that there had been some
kind of liaison between his then very young aunt and
Merriton. "A bit harsh, surely, Aunt Bea? I seem to
recall hearing at the time some talk of the wife becoming hysterical and vowing to kill herself if he left them

behind, and how they should all perish together, if perish they must."

"Oh, well, that was Arabella all over," her ladyship retorted, strengthening his suspicions. "She was my dearest friend, and I have to say that for all she was desperate to go with him, suicide was not in her nature. She simply knew how to twist him 'round her little finger. Any man of sense would have remained firm and left her and her child here in England where they were safely settled. She would not then have died in childbed in some foreign land with war and strife almost on the doorstep—she was never physically strong, you know—and the care of my poor godchild, Cressida, would not now have become such a pressing issue. He is sending her home and I am to take care of her, if you please. How Charles imagines I will cope, I do not know."

The earl had a feeling they were coming at last to the nub of things.

"Simple, dear ma'am," he said. "Hire a competent governess and pack them off to the country. You may have the use of Langley Manor if you so wish."

"That is more than generous of you, Alastair. But it would not answer. Only suppose you should wish to marry—for at eight-and-twenty it is high time you were considering it—you would not care to have the manor given over to strangers."

"My dear ma'am, in the unlikely event of my discovering some even remotely eligible female willing to take me to husband, I am persuaded that, given a choice, she would infinitely prefer the many delights of London to the wild windswept moors of north Yorkshire."

His voice had remained light, yet his expression warned her to proceed with care. Even so, with his best interests at heart, she felt compelled to speak her mind. "Stuff and nonsense! I wish you would not say such things. Of course you will marry. It is your duty to do so, and I am confident that there are any number of highly eligible young women only too willing to accept, were you to offer for them. If for no other reason, you must surely consider the succession."

"I try not to consider it, dear ma'am. The prospect is deeply depressing. What is more, I am quite certain that the world would not fall apart if there were one noble family the less."

"Of course it wouldn't. However, that is not the point. It is your family we are speaking of—you have a duty to the family name . . ."

But the earl had heard it all before. His aunt, an excellent woman in many ways was, once in full flow, famous for the length of her perorations. And since he had no wish to offend her, he had long since perfected the art of appearing to listen, in the certainty that a murmur of assent or appreciation now and again would fulfil all that was expected of him.

In this, he underestimated her.

The clock on the mantelpiece struck five, spelling blessed release. He rose to his feet without haste. "Forgive me, dear ma'am, but I am promised elsewhere."

"No forgiveness is needed, my boy. It is good of you to come at all. You cannot know how much I appreciate your taking time out of your busy life to listen to my troubles, to say nothing of your willingness to perform the occasional small service for me."

"It is little enough, Aunt Beatrice. I hope you know you may always count on me."

She fingered the rope of pearls adorning her ample bosom. "Splendid. I knew you would not let me down. My mind is much relieved.

"Now it simply remains to arrange a time."

A dreadful premonition seized him, driving all thought of Isabella from his mind. Could he have missed something of vital importance? "Time?" he queried.

"Naturally, I do not expect you to accomplish matters immediately. You will have commitments, as will dear Cressida. I daresay there will be any number of arrangements to be made before she can come to me."

Indignation overcame prudence as he cursed his wretched air-dreaming. "Aunt Beatrice, much as I appreciate your difficulty, you surely don't expect me to travel to Lisbon to rescue this godchild of yours? Good God, I know nothing about children—nor do I care to learn . . ."

"My dear boy! As if I would be so skimble-brained! That is all taken care of. Cressida will travel with a member of the embassy staff and his wife who are due home presently to visit a sick parent—somewhere in Devon, I believe, though that is neither here nor there. However, in the circumstances it would seem a great imposition to expect them to deliver the dear girl to my door. So it occurred to me that you might be so obliging as to meet Cressida off the ship and convey her to me here."

It was iniquitous—impossible! How could she possibly expect him to . . . Any number of objections sprang to his lordship's lips, only to wither away, unspoken, beneath her look of entreaty. He sighed and surrendered to the inevitable.

"I am, as always, your to command, dear aunt. So, when, exactly am I required to execute this trifling commission?"

The sarcasm was not lost on her, but she feigned innocence. "Oh, not for several weeks, dear boy. The Cresswells hope to leave Lisbon early next month, I believe." It was very quiet in the room when Alastair had gone. Lady Kilbride sighed and closed her eyes, unable any longer to hold her memories at bay. Charles Benedict Merriton had entered her life at a midsummer ball when she was a green girl, barely out and he a practised charmer, though she was then too dazzled to realize it.

"Enchanting," he had murmured when introduced by her father. He had smiled down at her in a way that made her foolish heart turn over and beat uncomfortably fast, and so loud that she was sure he must hear it. "Dare I hope that your dance card is not full, and that I may at some point be permitted to play Benedict to your Beatrice?"

That had been the start of it. In the weeks that followed he had courted her assiduously and the world became a magical place. She had even dared to dream. And then Arabella Fairburn, who was her dearest friend and was both beautiful and quite devoid of vanity, had arrived in town, and the moment she and Charles met, it became blindingly obvious that her own dreams had no substance in reality.

But time, so it is said, heals most things—not least of all the dreams of foolish adolescents. And in the fullness of time she had married Edgar, Viscount— later to be Earl—Kilbride, a kind and gentle man ten years her senior. It had been a happy marriage, and although they were not blessed with children, there were many compensations. With a small family estate in Yorkshire as well as the house in Mount Street, life was never dull. Indeed, they were at the very hub of society. When he had died quite suddenly of a seizure in his forty-seventh year she was devastated. The Yorkshire property went to a distant cousin, but she did not care. Life as she had known it, held no further attraction for her, and in spite of the efforts of good and caring friends, she had closeted herself in the Mount Street house, totally withdrawn from society.

Now, it seemed, all was to change and she scarcely knew how she was to cope.

Pale petals clung like late snowfall to the vehicles vying for space outside Sir Giles Milchester's residence in Berkeley Square as the earl maneuvered his lightly sprung phaeton with commendable ease amid the jostling vehicles and the muttered curses of the coachmen, all very much at odds with the balmy April evening. Beneath an awning footmen lined the carpeted front steps with lamps held aloft, and every window was ablaze with light.

"Stay close by, Henry," he said, tossing the reins to his groom. "I doubt I shall remain long."

"I'll be here, m'lord, never you fear."

In the brightly lit foyer, he surrendered his hat and cane to yet another footman and made his way unhurriedly toward the curving staircase, whence the steady hum of sound interspersed with music and laughter drifted down.

"Alastair, I declare I had almost given you up for lost." As he reached the head of the staircase, Lady Milchester, plump and overdressed in puce silk, hurried forward and tapped him playfully with her fan. "And so, I believe, had a certain young lady who has been forever watching the door."

"I fear you flatter me, ma'am."

"No, I promise you, dear boy. Now do go and put her out of her misery."

The earl lifted her hand to his lips. "Your wish is my command," he murmured, and strolled on into the brightly lit ballroom, leaving her ladyship with the oddest impression that, for all his impeccable good manners, she had somehow offended him.

Miss Isabella Devine was being plagued by a lovesick young subaltern when she saw the earl, and at once made her excuses to her companion with little regard for his feelings. The young man blushed scarlet and stepped back, stammering an incomprehensible apology for detaining her, which she scarcely stayed to hear. And when he saw the object of her swift flight, he knew that his cause was hopeless.

"My lord, I was beginning to think you had been otherwise detained!" Isabella declared as she reached

Alastair's side, using her prettily embellished fan to great effect as she smiled up at him.

"Not in the least. It is merely that I have a horror of being the first to arrive." He put up his glass. "You are looking remarkably lovely this evening," he murmured, and heard her catch her breath.

Indeed the compliment was no less than the truth, for her gown of white *mousseline de soi* clung to her slight figure, revealing almost as much as it concealed. The result was an intriguing mix of ingenue and woman of the world, the gown edged at its daringly cut neckline with tiny pink rosebuds, with more rosebuds nestling in her silver-fair hair. But there was nothing ingenuous about the simple gold chain that adorned her lovely neck. It held a glittering pear-shaped diamond which nestled invitingly in the hollow between her breasts like an open invitation.

Had she been less obvious, he might have been tempted to pursue his cause. But if ever he decided to succumb to her lures, it would be on his terms.

"That poor subaltern who is in thrall to you looked sadly chastened. Do I take it that you have spurned him?"

Her laugh tinkled on the air. "He is so young, and quite embarrassingly shy. I must find for him some little ingenue who will melt at the sight of his uniform."

Which is not in the least what the poor boy was hoping for, Alastair thought.

"May I join you?" a familiar voice murmured apologetically. "Or shall I be accused of spoiling sport?"

Alastair turned with something approaching relief. "Perry, I had not expected to see you here."

Peregrine Devenham shrugged his elegantly clad shoulders. "I almost didn't come. Fool of a valet mangled at least half of my cravats."

"Poseur," the earl retorted, but there was the hint of a smile lurking in his eyes, for Perry was a friend of long standing, and he knew, none better, that beneath the foppish exterior lurked an intelligent mind and a sometimes rapier wit.

"And how does our delightful hostess mean to entertain us this evening, I wonder?" Devenham mused.

"There is to be a concert, I believe," Isabella said swiftly, a trifle put out at being excluded from the conversation. "And dancing later for those who wish it." She fluttered her fan, her brilliant blue eyes issuing a tantalizing invitation which she sensed that this time he might be persuaded to accept. And as for later . . . well, later, anything might happen.

Chapter Two

It was early in March when Lady Kilbride received a letter from Cressida Merriton with the news that she hoped to leave Lisbon on the following Monday on one of His Majesty's ships. She perused the letter once more—"which should arrive in England within the month though much would depend on the weather." Her ladyship sent word to Alastair at once.

"It is most gratifying to note that Cressida continues to write a very pretty hand," her ladyship confided to him when he arrived. "It is not always so with young people, I believe."

The earl restrained the impulse to retort that her goddaughter's writing skills were of little interest to him, confining himself instead to discussing the practicalities. "There is the trifling matter of where she is to be met," he said with an irony that completely bypassed her.

Lady Kilbride consulted the letter again. "She makes mention of Portsmouth, which seems very likely, wouldn't you say?"

"And I am required to meet her there, and convey her to you, I suppose?"

The biting sarcasm appeared to escape his aunt. "Shall you mind? You young bucks seem to think nothing of travelling as many miles to witness some crude exhibition of pugilism, or the like, so I cannot suppose you will be greatly inconvenienced. I daresay it will be necessary to put up somewhere for a night, but Cressida will undoubtedly have some kind of maid or governess-companion, so all will be perfectly proper."

"As if that were the only consideration," he complained to Perry Devenham later that evening in White's. The club was quiet, with only a few elderly men gently dozing over their port, and from somewhere more distant, the occasional burst of laughter. "The devil of it is, apart from the total disruption of any plans I might have made, can you honestly see me bear-leading some chit of a schoolroom miss, Perry? Dammit, I shouldn't know what to say to her."

Devenham eyed his friend, slumped with careless elegance in his chair with his long legs stretched out before him, and chuckled. "And this from a fellow renowned for his ability to charm the fair sex," he drawled.

"That is quite a different matter. Charm don't come into it in this instance." Alastair waved an empty bottle at one of the waiters, who came at once to take it from him.

"Another of the same, Arthur."

"Yes, m'lord. At once, m'lord."

"Speaking of the fair sex," Devenham continued. "How goes it with the lovely Isabella?"

Alastair sighed. "A trifle tediously, if you must know. She is undoubtedly desirable, and yet . . ."

His friend eyed him quizzically. "Is there a difficulty? I would have thought her ripe for the plucking."

"That is the difficulty, dear boy. Truth to tell, the fair Isabella is becoming a trifle overeager, and where's the challenge in that? Can't answer for others, of course, but the thrill goes out of the chase if the quarry ain't putting up any kind of resistance."

It grieved Devenham to hear the note of cynicism in his friend's voice. He was not by nature malicious, but there were times when he wished Lady Alice Waring had never existed. But he only said quietly, "Ain't like you to complain. You don't know when you're well-off, dear old friend."

"Perhaps not," he agreed. "Could be I'm just blue-devilled over this wretched godchild of my aunt's." The waiter returned with the wine. "The club seems damnably quiet, this evening, waiter. Any decent play to be had?"

"A few young hotheads bent on throwin' their money away. None as'd prove a match for your skills, m'lord."

"Ah, well. So be it. I'm not really in the mood." The waiter bowed and retreated. "I suppose you wouldn't care for a rubber of whist, Perry? No, I can read your mind. Can't say I blame you. It'd be poor sport."

"So, when are you to have the doubtful pleasure of meeting this young godchild and conveying her to Lady Kilbride?"

"Ah, now there you have me. The whole affair is so deuced vague. As far as I can ascertain she is travelling on His Majesty's frigate, the *Sunderland,* which is due in Portsmouth two weeks or so from now, circumstances permitting. Which means I could be kicking my heels for days if she hits bad weather."

"Then I wish you luck, dear boy."

"Luck don't come into it," Alastair muttered morosely. "Unless the wretched girl changes her mind or succumbs to a fever."

But no such miracle prevailed, and the earl arrived in Portsmouth at the appointed time to find that the *Sunderland,* one among several recent arrivals, had already berthed. The dockside was a heaving, rowdy mass of humanity, with baggage spilling over in heaps at every turn, as he maneuvered his travelling chaise into one of the few remaining openings and tossed the reins to his coachman.

"Hold 'em steady, Henry," he said, as they skittered

nervously in the confined space. "I'll be as quick as I can."

"I have 'em safe, m'lord, never fear. It's you as'd best have a care, if you don't take it amiss me sayin' so . . . there's many 'ere as'd fleece you, soon as look at you."

"They can try," came the terse reply.

The earl negotiated his way through the crowds, scanning the assorted vessels for a glimpse of the *Sunderland*. A touch on his arm brought a swift instinctive reaction. Greatcoat swirling, he turned and seized the slim wrist. There was a gasp of pain, and he found himself looking into eyes that seemed startled rather than frightened, wide thickly fringed eyes, more green than grey beneath a stylish bonnet, from which one dark glistening curl had escaped.

"Milord!" she exclaimed. "You are hurting me."

"I'll hurt you more if you struggle." Around them the crowds swirled, though few eyed them curiously. As for Alastair, he was oblivious of anyone or anything except this brazen doxy. She was a little above average height, her head level with his shoulder, and the face lifted to him revealed strength rather than beauty, with a definite hint of wilfulness about the chin. His glance encompassed the exceedingly modish bronze green redingote in which he discerned the hand of an expert modiste, which suggested that in all probability she would have a rich protector. "And don't 'milord' me, my girl. I know your game. Give me one good reason why I shouldn't hand you over to the nearest constable?"

"You might end up looking a little foolish, I think."

He could swear she was amused, the baggage! And clearly someone had taught her to dress and speak well. But he was in no mood to play games. His grip tightened. "Enough of this nonsense . . ."

"I agree," she conceded swiftly. "It is nonsense, and the fault is entirely mine. I recognized you at once, of course, but how could I possibly expect you to remember me?"

For a moment he wavered, his mind grappling through past indiscretions. Surely they had not met—he had not . . . ? And then anger took over. "How, indeed? For you may be sure that if we had met, I would not have forgotten you."

"But then," she said demurely, "I was only eight years old at the time, my lord, and, green as I was, I thought you quite the most handsome gentleman I had ever seen."

Before he had time to collect his wits, a tall raw-boned woman hung about with several bandboxes and a portmanteau came bustling up, glared at him, and let forth an extraordinary tirade of reproof in the course of which the name, "Miss Merriton," figured, and suspicion immediately became fact. Which did little to soothe his temper.

His eyes raked her from head to toe, but this time they held a harsh glimmer of indignation bordering on disbelief. "You are Cressida Merriton?"

"I fear so, my lord." Sparkling white teeth trapped a full lower lip. "Forgive me. It was stupid and childish of me to tease you so. I can only attribute my misplaced levity to the insufferable tedium of the voyage."

Oh, the devil! He groaned inwardly. Aunt Beatrice, how could you have gulled me so? For this was no schoolroom miss. Cressida Merriton must be nearer twenty years than eighteen.

"We certainly seem to have been at cross-purposes," he said stiffly. "But my aunt gave me quite the wrong impression. As a result, I was expecting someone much younger."

"Oh dear!" She tried very hard to preserve an air of gravity. "Then I can understand how disconcerting all this must be for you. It is probably Pa's fault. He will persist in referring to me still as his little girl."

How like Charles Merriton, he thought. "No matter. This place is like bedlam, and the sooner we are out of it, the better. We have already wasted more time than enough." He glanced around. "I understood from Lady Kilbride that you were travelling with some people from the embassy?"

"The Cresswells—yes, indeed. They have been most kind, but I knew that they were anxious to get to Devon before nightfall—before we left Lisbon Mrs. Cresswell received news that her mother was failing rapidly—so I persuaded them that I would be quite safe with the nice lieutenant from the *Sunderland* until you came."

"How noble of you." He looked around. "And where is this gallant protector?"

"He will be here at any moment. He is supervising the safe transference of my baggage."

"And suppose I hadn't come to meet you?"

"That seemed very unlikely. But in that event, I would probably have consulted the ship's captain and the harbormaster or whoever—after which I would have repaired to the nearest reputable inn to await your arrival."

"How very resourceful of you," he remarked with cutting sarcasm. "Do you often flirt with danger?"

She seemed unmoved by his reaction. "Not intentionally. But Pa taught me long ago how to take care of myself, for as he warned me, one cannot be too careful."

"Quite." He wasn't sure if the sarcasm escaped her, or was deliberately being ignored. He continued, still tight-lipped, "And naturally you will have some kind of companion."

"I have my good maid, Jane Batty, here, who is a formidable protector. And, of course, the Cresswells were more than adequate company throughout the journey." They might have been discussing the weather. "So, since I was confident of being met, it

seemed quite unnecessary to burden myself with anyone else."

The earl did not attempt to hide his disapproval of
her light-minded ways, which was reflected in his
voice. "Then there is nothing to detain us once your
belongings are brought ashore."

Even as he spoke a young naval officer who was
clearly smitten with his young charge came hurrying
toward them, followed by a midshipman staggering
under the weight of yet another large portmanteau.

"Ah, Miss Merriton, here you are." One glance was
enough to establish that the young lady's companion—
a Corinthian of the first water—was known to her.
The lieutenant's eagerness diminished slightly. "You
have found your relation, I see."

"Thank you, yes, Mr. Pearson." She introduced the
two gentlemen. "The earl is not in fact a relation, but
his aunt is my godmother, and he most kindly agreed
to meet me and deliver me safely to her."

"Then you are fortunate indeed," the young lieutenant said, endeavoring to disguise his feeling of
envy.

The earl lifted his quizzing glass. "Is this the full
extent of your baggage, Miss Merriton?"

His sarcasm seemed totally wasted on her. "I believe so. Except . . ." She turned again to the young
lieutenant. "Where is Manuel? He is aware that he is
to bring Vitoria?"

Not another female! Alastair groaned inwardly.

But in this he was mistaken. The crowds hastily
drew aside to permit a young groom to lead forward
an elegant and distinctly lively pure white gelding.

"Isn't he beautiful?" Cressida exclaimed with pride,
as the horse pricked his ears and became skittish at
the sound of her voice. She made soothing noises and
gave him an affectionate pat. "When Pa bought him
for me, he had an unpronounceable Portuguese name,

so I renamed him after one of Lord Wellington's great battles."

Words momentarily failed the earl. "You cannot seriously expect me to convey your horse to London."

"Oh, Vitoria won't be any trouble. He has beautiful manners, and Manuel will ride him, and see to all his needs." Cressida saw the earl's brow crease once more into an awesome frown and pressed home her point. "I'm sorry, but I really had no choice. I couldn't bear to leave him behind to pine, and there is no guarantee that Pa will return to Lisbon . . ."

The earl knew that everyone was waiting in breathless expectation for his next utterance—and that he would be dubbed the vilest of villains if he refused to accept her horse along with all else. He looked up and encountered an unexpected look of pleading in her wide green eyes.

"Very well," he said shortly. "As long as your groom is prepared to keep up with us. I wait for no one."

"Nor would I expect you to, my lord," she returned with equal crispness. And then, meeting his eyes, her expression softened. "Thank you."

Cressida had the impression that he had decided what couldn't be cured must be endured. When, after journeying through some very pretty countryside, they eventually stopped for a change of horses, Lord Langley spent some moments in conversation with the farrier before returning to the coach.

"Would it inconvenience you greatly, Miss Merriton, if we made a brief diversion?" he said, settling himself opposite her.

"Not in the least," she replied. "I am well used to diversions."

He threw her a quizzical look. "I have a property close by which, according to the farrier here, is giving cause for some concern among the neighbouring tenants."

"Then it would be absurd to forgo the chance to investigate when you are so close."

He looked for sarcasm, but found none. With fresh horses they made good time and were soon turning in between a pair of classical stone gateposts and along a curving driveway, its edges rampant with perfumed honeysuckle which drew from Cressida a sigh of pleasure. The driveway eventually straightened out to reveal ahead of them a charming manor house, its windows looking out over what had once been impressive gardens, both of which as they drew closer showed obvious signs of neglect.

"Oh, what a shame!" she exclaimed. "Such a fine building, too!"

Lord Langley's muffled exclamation revealed the extent of his disgust.

"Had you no idea?" she ventured.

"None," he said abruptly. "Haven't been near the place in years. It never held particularly happy memories for me, and since the death of my parents I have been content to leave matters to an appointed agent."

"Well, it seems obvious to me that he has been grossly negligent in his duties."

"Quite." The earl climbed down and mounted the steps to tug impatiently at the bellrope, which came away in his hands. He swore softly and at the same moment was aware that his young companion had followed him. But his apologies were brushed aside with the assurance that she had heard far worse in her travels.

At first it seemed that no one would answer. But as he was about to raise his fist, the heavy oak door creaked open and a woman clad in a faded calico gown beneath a much stained apron peered out at them, muttering, "There e'nt no one home . . ." then, recognising her caller, "Oh, lork's a mercy! Is it you, m'lord?"

"It is," he said grimly, pushing the door wider so

that she was obliged to stumble backward. Cressida, following him across the threshold, was immediately aware of the chill dankness of the hall and an all-pervading odour of stale cooking and damp.

"Perhaps you would care to explain why I find the manor in this disgusting state, Mrs. Cantrell?" he suggested with ominous calm.

The woman shrank visibly and clutched at her filthy apron, her voice becoming a pitiful whine. "I've not been well for while now, m'lord. You've but to ask Mr. Cantrell . . ."

"Who must have been equally indisposed if the state of the grounds is anything to go by," he concluded with cold logic.

By now Cressida was beginning to feel almost sorry for the poor woman. She had managed a glimpse into one or two of the nearby rooms and could see that, in spite of the evident neglect, it had once been a charming house. And could be so again.

"However, you may tell your husband that he will be hearing from me very soon, via my agent," Lord Langley was concluding. "Good day, Mrs. Cantrell."

With this he turned on his heel and retraced his steps, as if he had forgotten Cressida entirely. She followed with no word spoken, except for directions to the driver, until they were on their way again.

Then Cressida could hold her tongue no longer. "Did you have to be so hard on the poor woman? She was clearly inadequate, but perhaps the blame was not entirely hers."

"I have no intention of apportioning blame until I know the whole," he said with a finality that warned her to proceed no further. And for the remainder of the journey a cool silence reigned.

The inn where the earl had made reservations for their overnight stay came as a welcome sight to all. The taproom was busy, but the landlord came hurrying to greet them, eager to usher them into his private parlor where a fire burned brightly. "Unless you'd like to repair to your rooms first, m'lord . . . to refresh yourselves." It was not often that his premises were honored with the gentry, and he was anxious to please.

"I think not. Unless . . ." He turned to Cressida. "Would you prefer to retire, Miss Merriton—maybe rest for a while?"

"Thank you. But I am perfectly happy to remain here in this cosy parlor." She glanced at Jane Batty, who stood guard near the door, never taking her eyes from her mistress. "However, perhaps my maid could be provided with food—a little broth, perhaps, and some bread and cheese would suffice, and a glass of porter. Jane, dear, go along with the inkeeper."

If the innkeeper considered it an odd way to deal with servants, he kept his thoughts to himself and beckoned the woman. "Come along with me, my wife'll see to you."

Jane Batty looked from her mistress to the earl with deep suspicion, but after a brief hesitation, she shrugged and prepared to follow the man from the room.

The question of Manuel and the horse had already been addressed, the innkeeper being quick to reassure his lordship that he would find the stables clean and dry—and that both horse and man would be well fed.

"There's no one else stayin' at present, m'lord, so you will be given every attention and privacy. You'll be hungry, I daresay, after your long drive, but my wife's fare is as good as you'll find anywhere hereabout. There's one of her famous raised mutton pies, and a dish of pigeons braised in ale. An' if that ain't to your likin', there's the best part of a cold ham, and an apple pie with a jug of cream to follow. 'Tis plain fare, but you won't get better, even in Lunnon Town . . ."

"Yes, yes, it all sounds fine," said the earl impatiently. "And a couple of bottles of your best claret." He turned to Cressida. "Would you care for some cordial?"

"Thank you," she said pleasantly, "but claret will suit me very well."

One eyebrow quirked. "As you will."

Later he watched his young charge through veiled lids as they sat at a table which positively groaned under the generous ministrations of the innkeeper's wife. Cressida had grown quiet during the meal, and despite her protestations that she was as fit as a flea, he suspected that the coach ride, preceded by the long sea journey, was beginning to take its toll. The wine appeared to revive her a little, and her appetite, though not large, was healthy enough to persuade the earl that a night's sleep would soon set her right.

Cressida was very much aware of his silent disapproval. They had not made the best of beginnings, and for that she must accept some of the blame. Except that she wasn't sure how to set things right without making bad worse. In the end she decided that this was neither the time nor the place to mend matters.

"I hope you won't feel you must stay to bear me company," Alastair said when they were later seated either side of a blazing fire. "After your long and probably less than comfortable voyage, followed by several hours on the road, you must be bone weary . . ."

"It is good of you to be concerned, but I am well used to travelling. Pa is such a restless creature and we were forever off on some ploy. I have never known him to flag, even at the end of the most tiring journey."

"And as his only child, you consider it your duty to emulate him?"

"Good gracious, no!" There was nothing inhibited

about her ripple of laughter. "There was never any question of it being a duty. I can honestly say that I have enjoyed every minute of our life together. Indeed, I longed to accompany him to France . . ."

"Which he would not have permitted, surely, with all the dangers involved?"

"Oh, that wouldn't have troubled Pa unduly, for it wouldn't have been the first time I had courted danger," she said calmly. "Only he had promised poor Mama on her deathbed that he would do everything to ensure that I made my come-out when I was eighteen. Which became an impossibility, of course, for when that particular birthday came around, the situation in the Peninsula put any question of returning to England out of the question. I was quite relieved, but he vowed that Mama would never forgive him if he didn't keep that promise just as soon as the situation changed. Which it now has. I would rather have gone with him to Paris, but with Boney on the run, and the seas less hazardous, he decided that the time had come. Which is why he wrote to Lady Kilbride."

The earl rocked back in his chair, his eyes half-closed, unreadable, as they seemed to take in every detail of her appearance. "Are you telling me that your father is relying on Lady Kilbride to arrange your come-out?"

"Yes, of course." Her eyes warmed with amusement. "Of course, the whole idea is absurd as I shall make clear to her, for I am nearer twenty than eighteen, and I suspect he was motivated more by the fear that a grown daughter might cramp his style with all the pretty Parisian ladies, than that the spectre of Mama might come back to haunt him." She broke off as he let out a great, seemingly unfeeling shout of laughter. "Really, my lord. I don't see . . ."

"That much is self-evident, Miss Merriton," he replied, as his chair thudded back to the floor. "For I have to tell you that, much as she might wish to oblige, it would be impossible. My aunt, you see, has long since become a recluse. In fact, I doubt if she has been out of the house more than a dozen times in the last four years."

Chapter Three

"My dear Cressida, at last!" Lady Kilbride exclaimed. "But, my goodness, how you have grown. You are quite a young lady. And so elegant I would scarcely have known you."

Cressida's eyes were alight with laughter as she bent to kiss her godmother's cheek, although she was secretly dismayed to see that Lord Langley had not exaggerated the change in her, for she bore very little likeness to the vivacious lady of happy memory.

"It would be wonderful if it were otherwise, dear ma'am, for I cannot have been much more than twelve when I left England—a gangling creature, all arms and legs. No, pray do not attempt to get up," she added as the old lady struggled to rise. "But I remember you quite clearly, and you have scarcely changed at all."

"Nonsense." She sighed. "That is tipping the butter boat with a vengeance, for I am grown old and fat, and never leave the house."

"Well, I mean to change all that, you see if I don't," Cressida said, and was puzzled to note her godmother's sudden look of apprehension. She looked to the earl for some kind of guidance, but he seemed not to have noticed, so she stripped off her gloves and looked around her with quiet concern. She had not immediately noticed the figure in the far corner, sitting bolt upright and very still in a most uncomfortable-looking chair. Lady Kilbride immediately became flustered and introduced her as Miss Agatha Cheam, her companion.

"Miss Cheam has been with me for several years," her ladyship continued, striving with scant success to inject some genuine degree of enthusiasm into her voice. "Indeed, I sometimes wonder what I should have done without her."

A great deal more than you would appear to be doing now, Cressida thought. Glancing across at the earl, she could deduce nothing from his expression, but his silence spoke volumes. "Well, now you have me," she said. "And we shall have so much to talk about. His lordship tells me that Pa rather misled you, which does not surprise me. I hope you don't consider my coming a dreadful imposition."

"Oh, my dear, nothing could be further from the truth! I could not be happier. Miss Cheam, could you perhaps go and ask Martha to arrange for cook to make tea?" She turned to Cressida. "Unless you would prefer to rest. You must be worn-out, after that horrid and hazardous long journey. I cannot understand what your father was about, allowing you to come."

"Tea would be lovely," she said, if only to get rid of that Friday-faced woman for five minutes. "And I am not in the least bit tired. His lordship engaged rooms for us at a very pleasant inn yesterday. We enjoyed an excellent meal, and I slept the night through like a baby. Is that not so, my lord?"

He gave her a somewhat enigmatic look. "I cannot vouch for the latter," he murmured, experiencing a curious feeling of satisfaction as she blushed, "but Miss Merriton seems to have been in excellent spirits throughout, in spite of the long journey."

"As for danger, our navy is better equipped than any to deal with it. I have been in far more dangerous situations in Spain."

"I thought you had been in Lisbon? You cannot

mean that Charles ever allowed you to accompany him into danger? I cannot believe he would be so uncaring."

"Not uncaring, dear ma'am. It was I who sometimes insisted on accompanying him. Life in Lisbon could become tediously trivial."

"Goodness," Lady Kilbride exclaimed. "What it is to be young. However, you are here now. Alastair, I'm sure Cressida will not object if you would be so good as to draw up that chair for her. I think you will find it quite comfortable, my dear."

Cressida had been looking 'round her as they conversed, and what she saw disturbed her. She remembered Lord Langley's remarks about his aunt having become a recluse, and everything she now saw seemed to confirm this. The room was fairly comfortably furnished but it was much too gloomy and cluttered, exuding a faint decaying odor of past splendors—rather like its present incumbent. And that awful companion. It suddenly became clear to her that she had been directed to this place for a purpose.

"Do you know," she said, "I can distinctly remember coming here as a child. You always kept a little bowl of lavender—you still do, I see."

Lady Kilbride flushed with pleasure. "Fancy you remembering that!"

The earl had remained near the door watching with a somewhat jaundiced eye as his aunt struggled to adjust her preconceived image of this goddaughter of hers who had left England as a child and returned now as a stylish, self-possessed young woman. He found himself wondering how they would deal together, as different as they were.

"Will you stay for tea, Alastair?" his aunt enquired, as Miss Cheam returned, laboring under the weight of a laden tray.

"Not for me, Aunt Beatrice," he said hastily. "With

your permission, I shall leave the two of you to reminisce to your hearts' content."

"Very well, dear boy. I quite understand."

He bent to kiss his aunt's cheek and turned to Cressida. "Miss Merriton, I leave you in my aunt's good care."

"Thank you, my lord. You have been very kind"—her eyes crinkled into a mischievous smile—"not least in offering to take care of my dear Vitoria, until I can make other arrangements."

He inclined his head. "My stables are large," he said casually. "You have but to send word when you wish to ride him, and I'll have a groom bring him 'round."

"I usually like to ride early in a morning, but I don't wish to be any trouble."

"Tomorrow morning, then? About eight o'clock?"

Cressida was beginning to recognize that certain glint in his eyes. He was challenging her—attempting to call her bluff. She was sure of it as he added blandly, "Or do you need time to recover from your journey?"

Her chin lifted a fraction as she smiled up at him. "Certainly not. Eight o'clock would be splendid."

"Your horse?" Lady Kilbride had been listening in amazement. "You have brought a horse all the way from Portugal?"

"I suppose it must seem very odd of me, but what else was I to do? I couldn't bear to leave him behind. The poor boy would have pined most dreadfully—and, most likely, so should I. So, with Pa bound heaven knows where, and no certainty when or if I shall ever return to Lisbon, there seemed little alternative."

"I see." There was an element of surprise in her ladyship's voice that was not missed by the earl. "I still keep a stable, though I now have no need of one. But that could soon be remedied. Meanwhile, you may consider yourself honored that Alastair is to stable your horse. He is in general very particular."

"Nonsense," said the earl, turning away with a swirl of his greatcoat. "One horse here or there makes little difference."

As the door closed behind him, Lady Kilbride said with a distinct twinkle in her eyes, as the unexpected possibility of bridals began to stir in her plump bosom, "Well, I must say I have not seen Alastair so conciliatory in a long time. Do you know, my dear Cressida, I think your visit might prove to be providential in more ways than one."

The clock in the dining room had barely finished striking the hour on the following morning when the repeated pealing of the doorbell brought Martha hobbling into the hall, clutching her shawl about her shoulders.

"Be still, will you? I'm coming as fast as I can." She paused for breath. "Though where that lazy good-for-nothing, Paul's got to, I don't know. I'm not fit for answerin' doorbells at this hour of the mornin'— Oh, gracious me!" she exclaimed, opening the door wider. "Lord Langley! I'd clean forgotten we was to expect you at this hour. I daresay Miss Merriton'll be down directly. Her ladyship's not about yet, but you'd not expect her to be, o' course. Come in, do, m'lord, an' don't take no notice of me an' me rheumatics."

"You should let the young ones do the running about, Martha," he said, removing his hat and stepping into the hall.

"An' so I would, m'lord—gladly, if I could make them mind me. Meg will be upstairs with her ladyship, o' course, for that Miss Cheam's neither use nor ornament, beggin' yer pardon, m'lord, an' Cook's busy with breakfast, but as for that young good-for-nothin', Paul . . ."

"A lad like that needs a firm hand. You're too soft with him, Martha."

"So what would you advocate, my lord?" a familiar voice enquired. "A touch of the switch, perhaps?"

He looked up to see Cressida Merriton coming round the curve in the stair. She was wearing a riding habit of dark green cloth with collar and epaulets picked out in black braiding, and half boots in black leather. Her chestnut curls were tied back with green ribbon beneath a neat black hat, very much à la Hussar.

"The switch has its corrective merits, if all else fails," he replied smoothly, though still with that certain look in his eyes. "You are looking remarkably spry for someone who has spent so long in travelling. I thought you might have changed your mind and be still abed."

She refused to rise to the bait. "Goodness, I hope I am not so poor spirited. Especially as it is such a beautiful morning—much the best time to ride."

"I imagine your Vitoria agrees with you," he said blandly, ushering her out into the fresh spring day. "He is more than eager to shake the fidgets out of his legs. In fact, Stebbings, my groom, has had the devil's own job containing him. I hope you won't find him too much of a handful."

Cressida threw him a derisive look and walked across to where Vitoria waited impatiently, caracolling, throwing back his head and shaking his silky mane, so that it took Stebbings all his time to hold him.

"I'd have a care, miss—beggin' your pardon," he warned, keeping a strong grip on the snaffle. "Got it on him, good an' proper, 'e has."

"Small wonder, after the trials of a long sea journey and having to spend two nights in strange surroundings. You should have let Manuel bring him."

"An' so I would have, miss, an' welcome," he said grudgingly, "but the lad was clear wore-out—dead to the world."

Vitoria had pricked up his ears at the sound of his mistress's voice and as she ran a hand along his flank and made soothing noises, he whinnied and turned to nudge her, soft as a baby.

"That's a good boy," she murmured, adding a few foreign-sounding words. "I know everything is very strange, but you'll be fine once we get into the park."

"Well, I never," muttered Stebbings. "Who'd have thought it."

The earl had been standing back watching, narrow-eyed, ready to move if necessary, and was immoderately irritated to find her more than competent to cope with the high-couraged animal. Now he came forward. "Shall we go?" he said with a hint of impatience.

"Certainly, my lord, if you will be so good as to hand me up."

The park was deserted, except for the occasional lone rider in the far distance. The sun was already high enough to send shards of light filtering through the leaves of the trees as they shivered slightly in the breeze, and dew lay like a film of ice across the wide sweeps of grass either side of the path.

Cressida turned eagerly to the earl, who had not spoken since they entered the park gates. "What a piece of luck to have all this space to ourselves, and Vitoria longing to shake the fidgets out of his legs." Her eyes sparkled with mischief. "Come—I'll race you to the far end."

"No! Wait!" He was too late. She was away and he had no alternative but to give chase. But even in his anger, a tiny corner of his mind was forced to acknowledge, "By God, she can ride!"

He had no choice but to follow, and even riding full out, he only drew level with her as they reached the far end.

"That was wonderful!" she declared breathlessly.

"It was also reckless and foolish in the extreme, riding like a hoyden," he snapped, his anger further inflamed by the sight of her laughing, glowing face. "Don't ever do it again."

"Gracious, I believe you are miffed. I had not thought you would be such a poor loser . . ."

"It is not a question of winning or losing." He ground the words out. "It is an unwritten rule, which you flout at your peril."

"But surely I am not the only one to have given way to temptation, especially at this hour of the morning." Her glance swept as far as the eye could see. "The park is deserted. I would not have attempted it, had matters been otherwise."

Far from mollifying him, the truth of her observation served merely to inflame his already exacerbated temper. Her eyes were very green and bright with righteous indignation. His were grey and implacable.

"I have said my piece. If you choose to ignore my advice, on your own head be it." He wheeled his horse. "Shall we continue?"

Well, really! she thought.

They rode without speaking at a decorous pace. Cressida glanced at him and found his profile proud and unyielding. "Oh, come—was it really so terrible?" she asked, unable to bear the silence any longer. "After being for so long confined on board ship, you must surely allow that the temptation was irresistible."

"I have said all I wish to say on the matter."

"Well, I have not, my lord. For one thing I cannot abide is bad feeling. So, much as it grieves me to forsake my principles—and in order to preserve some precious unwritten rule of etiquette—you may inform anyone who might have witnessed my hoydenish behavior that I am your aunt's goddaughter newly come to London and ignorant of your ways."

"Now you are being ridiculous," he said abruptly. "This time no harm was done. But if you do not wish to be branded as a hoyden, you will do well to restrain your natural inclinations if you should ride here later in the day, especially during the Season, and most especially during the Grand Strut . . ." He glanced across and saw she was puzzled. "Did your father never tell you about that particular quirk of our very particular society? Each afternoon in early summer, weather permitting, the fashionables take the air, all eager to outdo one another with their fine clothes and array of carriages, and even more eager to discover who is cutting who . . ."

Her trill of laughter broke the stillness. "I don't believe . . . oh, surely not!"

"You may laugh, Miss Merriton, but in London during the Season, reputations can be made or destroyed in an afternoon."

"How extraordinary! And I had been supposing that everyone would be rather dull and stuffy. I had no idea that it was likely to be so diverting."

His profile gave little away, and Cressida wasn't sure if he was still annoyed. But his comments had put her in mind of something she had resolved to ask him. Now might not be the best time, but then no time would be ideal, and it was not in her nature to fudge difficult issues.

"With regard to the Season, my lord—I wanted to ask you about Lady Kilbride. Clearly Pa could have had no idea that she had become so reclusive or he would not have asked her to sponsor me. Either that, or he did not make his wishes clear, which would not at all surprise me for he has a habit of dashing off personal letters in a very care-for-nothing way."

Lord Langley could have said much about her parent's care-for-nothing ways, but he confined himself to a noncommittal, "If you say so. I am entirely ignorant of any specific arrangements."

Cressida was determined not to allow his apparent disinterest to put her off. "I doubt there were any. I suppose Pa had some absurdly quixotic idea of fulfilling Mama's wishes, but I would as lief have stayed where I was, for I had become quite useful to him."

"Useful?"

"As a kind of secretary, I suppose, when delicate negotiations were required. Occasionally he needed someone he could trust implicitly, and he reckoned I had more good common sense than most of the wet-behind-the-ears subalterns that were foisted upon him to fulfil that role. Also, there were occasions when he reasoned that the presence of a young woman would pose less of a threat. Certainly people seemed to respond more cooperatively."

Had her father been anyone else, the earl would have dismissed these extraordinary revelations as so much air-dreaming. But he knew enough of Charles Merriton to suspect that every word was true.

"What a life you have led," he said dryly. "I wonder he could bear to be deprived of your services."

She laughed. "Oh, well, as to that, I suspect his crisis of conscience concerning my future was triggered by Lord Wellington having need of him in Paris. I could have gone with him, of course, but bearing in mind his penchant for the ladies, I suspect that the presence of a daughter of marriageable age might prove an embarrassing encumbrance."

The earl laughed aloud. "You are too young to be such a cynic."

"Not a cynic, my lord—a realist."

"Good God! That is worse. Realism is in short supply during the London Season. I hope you will not find life in London unconscionably tedious."

She could not fail to note the hint of sarcasm, but resolved to ignore it. "Oh, I don't think I will. There is plenty to be done. But, following on what you told me about Lady Kilbride—and indeed, what I immediately observed only too clearly for myself, I have not as yet decided how best to resolve her problem."

"In what way?"

"Well, clearly I have to convince her that making my formal curtsy to society like some little ingenue would be quite absurd when I have been attending balls in Lisbon for some considerable time, but much as she might long to be relieved of such a responsibility, I fear she will attempt to screw up her courage in order to fulfil what she sees as a duty to my late mother."

She had read the situation with remarkable clarity. The earl was intrigued in spite of himself to see how, if at all, she meant to resolve it. "And do you have a solution to your dilemma?"

"Well, I could simply tell her that I felt unable to face all the fuss, which would perhaps solve the problem, but might not salve her conscience."

"Or?" he murmured.

Her hesitation was momentary. "Or I could take Lady Kilbride in hand—persuade her to abandon her self-imposed isolation and resume her place once more in society. Then I would be happy to be introduced into society simply as her guest."

He threw her a highly quizzical look. "Brave words, Miss Merriton, but you don't know what it is you attempt. She may struggle to fulfil that misplaced sense of duty you seem so keen to dismiss, but she has been too long out of the world! The plain truth is, I fear Aunt Beatrice is by now beyond help."

"Oh, how poor-spirited of you to write her off so lightly!"

"Not lightly, I assure you."

Cressida feared she had offended him, for whatever his faults, he was clearly fond of his aunt. "I'm sorry," she said. "That was unthinking of me. But, unless you have reason to think it might harm her, I mean to try just the same."

"Such optimism! I only hope you may succeed where I failed, though I doubt it, short of a small miracle."

But you will be piqued if I do succeed, she thought, her mind already busy. The first thing she must do was to rid her godmother of that awful companion. She hadn't yet decided how best to go about it, but get rid of her, she would. They rode in silence for a while. It was Cressida who finally broke it.

"I was wondering, my lord—is Temple Bar very far from here?"

He shot her a frowning look. "What can you possibly want with Temple Bar?"

"That, if you will forgive my saying so, is neither here nor there." She saw he was about to take issue, and being anxious to avoid further argument, said, "If you must know, I need to see Mr. Pargeter, my father's man of business, whose premises are situated there. Because one cannot go on comfortably without money. And there are any number of things I may require."

"Nonsense. Aunt Beatrice is a wealthy woman, though she don't appear so. And if I know her, she will already be planning to lavish some of that wealth on you."

Cressida's chin lifted and he saw at once that he had said the wrong thing.

"It is very kind of her, but quite unnecessary. Pa was adamant that I should not be a charge on Lady Kilbride, which is why, before he left Lisbon, he gave me a letter to present to a Mr. Pargeter at his bank at Temple Bar, with instructions to advance me such funds as I might require."

"Your father is a very trusting man."

The gelding skittered slightly as one of Cressida's spurs jabbed his side. She leaned forward to soothe him, indignation overcoming caution as she retorted, "Not trusting. He knows I won't outstrip the budget. In fact, there was a time when he would have been in a poor way without me." She hesitated, but something—a need to make him understand, perhaps, drove her on. "The thing is, you see, Pa has many excellent qualities. But prudence is not one of them. His great weakness is vingt-e-un, and mostly he wins. But after Mama's death a little over three years ago—" I should not be telling him this, she thought as her throat grew tight—it is being disloyal to Pa. But once having begun, she found it impossible to stop. "I grew up rather quickly. The fact is," she continued, fixing her gaze on a nearby beech tree ahead of her, newly burgeoning, "he rather went to pieces for a short while after losing Mama, whom he adored and who was his sheet anchor, together with the son he had always longed for. As a result he . . . he drank too much and gambled away a great deal of money. If I had not finally persuaded him to let me take charge of our day-to-day finances, I dare not think what might have happened." A shaft of sunlight appeared to fragment into shards of light as tears threatened, and there was a rawness in her voice that could not be hidden.

The earl, moved in spite of himself, tried to visualise a rather younger Cressida struggling to take on duties ill suited to her years, knowing she could never replace that longed-for son. "Surely your father could have engaged someone to manage his affairs?"

This provoked in her a slightly choked laugh. "Quite probably. Except that he wouldn't have heeded him. But he could not deny me. And I knew that if I could just get him over the worst, he would come about."

"And did he?"

"Oh, yes. It took a little while, but as the war began to turn in our favor, he had other, more pressing matters to consider, and in a remarkably short time he had more than recouped his losses and was almost his old self again."

By this time they had reached the park gates. She dashed one gauntleted hand impatiently across her face. "I'm sorry, my lord. I cannot imagine how I came to treat you to such a pathetic scene, let alone give you quite the wrong impression of my father, who is a good and generous man."

Her father's penchant for gambling was not unknown to the earl. Within the portals of White's and Watier's he was but one of many. But he only said, "I am well aware of his fine qualities. As for the rest, you are too hard on yourself, Miss Merriton. I suspect you are suffering, among other things, from the delayed effects of your journey. You would have done better to sleep on this morning instead of rising so early."

"Perhaps."

"No perhaps about it." He hesitated, then heard himself saying, "If you are determined to visit this Mr. Pargeter—and if you would not construe it as a patronizing gesture on my part, I am more than willing to convey you to Temple Bar when you are able to arrange a time."

"You! Are you sure?" Cressida shot him a surprised look, then bit her lip. "I'm sorry. That must have sounded ungracious. But you must not think I mean to make a convenience of you."

"My dear young lady, when you know me better, you will realize that I seldom do anything I don't wish to do."

Chapter Four

It had taken Cressida but a short time in her godmother's company to realize that the earl had not
exaggerated in asserting that Lady Kilbride was completely out of touch with the real world. Though still
the kindly lady of distant memory, she had been for so
long cocooned in that once elegant, but now overfilled
shabby and stuffy room, with only the joyless Miss
Cheam for company, that in consequence she had become one with her surroundings.

"I cannot bear to see her so reduced," she told Lord
Langley as he drove her home from a very satisfactory
visit to Mr. Pargeter's banking premises at Temple
Bar. "My coming may have given her pleasure, but
the more I am with her, the more I become aware
that she has allowed herself to dwindle into a shocking decline."

"I couldn't agree more. After Kilbride's death some
years ago, she withdrew from the world, and has remained so ever since, despite concerted efforts from
those friends who still care for her. I have tried many
times to motivate her without success. Perhaps your
coming will have a beneficial effect, though by now
the task would appear hopeless."

"That is the philosophy of a defeatist. Oh, I am not
in any way denigrating your attempts," she assured
him, as his brows drew together. "I am aware that
you have been very caring. It shows in her voice whenever she speaks of you."

The earl threw her a sanguine look. "I do what I can, but she appears content to remain in a kind of limbo."

"But that is a shocking waste of a life! Why, she cannot be above five-and-forty, for all that she dresses as a relict, which is quite absurd. Why, I daresay that with a few new gowns and someone to arrange her hair more becomingly, she might still be quite a handsome woman."

"Undoubtedly," he murmured dryly. "But convincing her of that fact would seem to be beyond anyone's capability. Believe me, I have tried—we have all tried—to no avail."

"Well, a way will have to be found to persuade her to return to the real world," Cressida declared with spirit. "For I cannot bear to see her so reduced."

"And you intend to achieve this miracle?" the earl murmured.

"I doubt it will require anything quite so drastic as a miracle—simply a degree of resolution." She turned a radiant smile on him. "You know, I wasn't at all keen on the idea of coming back to England, but now I see that it was meant."

"Good God! Don't tell me you are one of those incorrigible managing females! I begin to feel almost sorry for Aunt Beatrice."

"Well, you need not, I assure you," she retorted with a toss of her head. "Sometimes people require a push in the right direction, but I have never hurt anyone. I realize of course that it will require a great deal of ingenuity and resolution, but there is nothing so diverting as a challenge. And you needn't fear, for I shall be very discreet. For a start I mean to get rid of that awful Cheam woman . . ."

"The devil you do!" The earl's hands inadvertently tightened on the reins, causing his high-couraged pair to jib so that he was obliged to give his whole attention to calming them down. "I strongly advise you to do nothing so ill considered. Cheam may not be to your taste, but she is better than no one at all, and someone must be there when you have moved on to other climes."

"I cannot agree. If I can persuade my godmother to look outward instead of inward, she will have no need of me or Miss Cheam. And a way must be found, for one can almost see any hint of pleasure draining away from her whenever that awful woman is present."

The earl was surprised and not a little peeved that she, in a matter of days, had picked up on something he should have noticed for himself. "I won't deny that Aunt Bea is more depressed when Cheam is around, but . . ."

"Well, there you are. Even you have noticed. That quite decides the matter. Perhaps," she murmured, "we could hire someone to kidnap the woman and spirit her away to become a companion to another lonely widow lady somewhere deep in the country."

"Such ruthlessness. I almost begin to pity Cheam," he said. "But I advise you to have a care. Playing God—meddling in other people's lives—can have disastrous consequences."

"Only if it is done without love. And I mean to take the greatest care. To begin with, I shall persuade her to take a short drive at quiet times, and later, to accompany me on little shopping expeditions—from what she said, I assume she no longer keeps a carriage, but that can soon be remedied. In fact, I am thinking of buying a phaeton or perhaps a curricle for my own use . . ." She ignored his murmured "Good God!" "Though that would not do for her, of course."

"If you are serious, I will provide a suitable carriage," he said firmly.

"Splendid. Also, I might perhaps drop a few subtle hints about buying some new curtains for her salon. Her present ones are shockingly gloomy." This met with a pregnant silence. "Which reminds me, I shall have need of a skilful dressmaker with an eye for fashion, a sense of style, and a sympathetic disposition. Would you happen to know of such a one?"

He shot her a look of disbelief. "My dear Miss Merriton, you expect too much of me. Whatever gave you the notion that I might be equipped to offer you such a recommendation?"

Her laughter had a refreshing ring of spontaneity. "It's not a notion, my lord. Call it rather a certain degree of observation which has led me to suppose that the more discriminating gentlemen of fashion are very much the same all the world over, and know a great deal more than they should about any number of things, including the more intimate details of ladies' fashions, though some may be more discerning than others. In Lisbon all was accomplished with the greatest decorum, but the gentlemen knew a great deal about what went on just the same, and I would imagine that London differs little in that respect."

"It seems to me that you also know a great deal too much, my girl," he said in crushing tones that seemed to leave her quite unmoved.

"Perhaps. I suppose that it served as a kind of defense against boredom. Life was very restricted for those of us who were insatiably curious, whilst still being of an age to be denied the many pleasures enjoyed by our elders. In consequence we would often resort to eavesdropping on servants' gossip and probably learned more than we should in the process, even if we didn't always fully understand what was said."

The earl was silent for so long that Cressida supposed her outspokenness had shocked him and, being unsure how to put matters right, fell silent.

Quite how matters might have been resolved she was never to know, for even as she pondered the problem, her companion was hailed by a young exquisite riding toward them on a very fine chestnut hunter.

"Thought it was you, Alastair," murmured this pink of the *ton,* drawing abreast of them.

"I hadn't expected to see you abroad at this hour, Perry."

"I know. Deuced bird began shrieking outside my window at some unearthly hour. Only one course open to me—summon up the blood and take the air."

Cressida smiled at the absurdity and found the young man smiling sleepily in return before turning in gentle enquiry to his friend.

"You remember I told you about Aunt Beatrice's godchild," the earl reminded him. "Miss Merriton, may I introduce a very good friend of mine, Mr. Peregrine Devenham."

"The young lady from Lisbon. Delighted to meet you, ma'am." Not by so much as a flicker of an eye did the fashionable young buck betray his surprise on discovering that she bore no relation to the much-anticipated schoolroom miss, as he swept his hat off and inclined his head. "Alastair did tell me you were to visit Lady Kilbride, but he failed to mention what a charming young lady we were to have among us for the Season."

"You are very kind, Mr. Devenham," she murmured, her mouth curving in a smile of pure pleasure. "Though I doubt his lordship shares your delight."

"Oh, I leave all that kind of thing to Perry," the earl said repressively. "He's a great one for tipping the butter boat. Miss Merriton is in need of a good dressmaker, Perry. Do you have any suggestions?"

"Of course," the young man murmured. "Only one worthy of serious consideration. You must go to Madame Fanchon in Conduit Street."

"Thank you." She turned to the earl, her eyes brimming with laughter. "What did I tell you? Discriminating gentlemen of fashion always know." And then to Mr. Devenham, who looked slightly bemused, "I am much obliged to you, sir. I shall take your advice just as soon as I can persuade my godmother to accompany me."

This seemed so unlikely as to cause the young man to glance across at his friend.

"Miss Merriton is determined to restore Aunt Beatrice to her former self. Not only that—she means to remove Miss Cheam."

"The devil she does!" Mr. Devenham transferred his attention to Cressida. "Splendid idea. Only met the woman once, and she aroused a deep feeling of depression in me. I wish you luck, ma'am."

"I have tried to impress upon Miss Merriton that my aunt won't be cajoled into any such venture," said the earl with a shrug.

"And I have avowed that I can be very determined," Cressida said. "So, we shall see who prevails."

"Tricky situation. Do her ladyship a power of good, of course. I shall await the outcome with interest, Miss Merriton." His horse was growing restive. "Must go. Agamemnon needs to shake the fidgets out of his legs. I shall repair to the park to reflect on the beauties of nature." He doffed his hat. "Meet again soon, I trust," he said, and rode away.

"What a very odd young man," Cressida said, as he disappeared from view. "But very likeable."

"He's a good friend," the earl said. "Don't let that air of indolence fool you, Miss Merriton. There is much more to Perry than meets the eye."

Cressida returned to the house in Mount Street full of resolution. Lady Kilbride, listening to her goddaughter's account of her morning out, wondered how she had passed her days before the child had come to her, for already the house seemed full of life. As for Cressida's most recent venture, it seemed extraordinary, not to say decidedly odd, that one so young should be concerned with money matters, let alone go visiting places of business, even accompanied as she was by someone as respectable and knowledgeable as Alastair. But from what she could make out, Cressida had found it a thoroughly enjoyable experience.

It was only when her goddaughter brought up the subject of visiting a dressmaker that she felt the first stirrings of unease. She looked round her comfortable room, and said with a hint of panic in her voice, "Oh, I don't think . . . that is, you must not consider it at all necessary to be patronizing some strange and probably ruinously expensive vendeuse, my dear. I have an excellent woman—a Mrs. Carter—who comes to the house whenever I have need of her, and she will make whatever one wishes at a fraction of the cost."

In her corner Miss Cheam stirred. "She is also sensible and proficient. Knows just what her ladyship's needs are."

Cressida longed to wring the woman's scrawny neck, but knew she must choose her words carefully. "The thing is, dear ma'am," she continued as if the companion had not spoken, "I had been so looking forward to visiting a really stylish modiste. Proficiency is not everything." She shot a look at Miss Cheam. "There is also elegance, imagination. I have often heard ladies discussing the rival merits of their favorite salons and it always sounded such fun. And then by coincidence we met that nice Mr. Devenham this morning and he has recommended one who sounds exactly right."

She had hoped to reassure her godmother, but her words seemed to have quite the opposite effect.

"Dear me. You don't think, perhaps . . . that is to say, Peregrine Devenham is a charming young man, as well as being the kindest of creatures. And it is said that his own dress can hardly be faulted, though I confess it is not entirely to my taste." There was a hint of desperation in her ladyship's voice. "But as to recommendations—he surely cannot be accounted an expert on what a lady requires?"

"Do you not think so, ma'am?" Cressida chuckled.

"He seemed extremely knowledgeable to me. Oh, do let us visit this modiste that he recommends. It will be such an adventure."

Lady Kilbride felt her heart flutter and miss a beat. Cressida sounded so eager, yet the mere thought of venturing beyond the safe haven of home immediately threatened to bring on one of her turns.

"My dear, would you be so kind as to pass me my smelling bottle? So foolish of me, I know, but I suddenly feel quite faint."

The corner chair creaked. Miss Cheam saw her moment and seized it. "I knew this would happen. Now see what you have done," she admonished sharply, hurrying forward with the salts. "Her ladyship is not fit for such goings-on."

"That is absolute rubbish, Miss Cheam," Cressida said, turning on her. "My godmother has been allowed to dwindle into a mere shadow of herself, and you have clearly encouraged her. But I shall not allow you to do so any longer."

"Well, really!" The woman turned, scarlet-faced, to Lady Kilbride. "Madam, am I to be spoken to in such a fashion?"

"Oh dear . . . I don't . . . I am not . . ." Her godmother's frail voice trembled as she grasped at the smelling bottle and inhaled deeply.

Miss Cheam seized the moment. "My dear ma'am! You are distressed. Do allow me assist you to your room. This has clearly been too much for you." She turned a vitriolic glance on Cressida. "I hope you are now satisfied. The young can be quite cruelly thoughtless."

"That is nonsense! There is nothing wrong with my godmother, though I suspect you have persistently contrived to convince her otherwise. So I suggest it would be much better if you were to go to your room, and quickly, before you make matters worse." For a few highly charged moments they faced one another, and Miss Cheam, realizing that her employer was by now too confused to lend her support, recognized the imminence of defeat and was the first to look away.

"Very well. I shall go, for my poor nerves are all of a whirl. I must take some physic."

"Oh, dear, poor Miss Cheam." Lady Kilbride pressed her handkerchief against her mouth, and murmured as the door closed, "Do you not think perhaps you were a little harsh?"

"Only as harsh as was necessary. The woman is a killjoy." Her godmother was clearly upset, yet, sympathetic though she might be, Cressida refused to give up so easily. She pulled up a footstool and sat with her hands clasped round her knees.

"Dearest ma'am," she began, "I am only too aware that I have been thrust upon you by Papa in the most cavalier way, which is not unlike him, sad to say. And I can see that in many ways my being here has set you all on end . . ."

"Oh, no, my child! Never say that—don't even think it!" Her ladyship fumbled for her handkerchief. "Your presence is a constant joy to me. You can have no idea . . . it is simply that I have grown accustomed to living very quietly since . . ." She pressed the handkerchief to her mouth.

"I do understand," Cressida exclaimed. "Believe me, I have no desire to upset you. And, for all Pa's impetuous ways, I am certain that had he realized your present state of mind, he would never have thrust me upon you. But I am here now, and I ask nothing of you but the pleasure of your company. I have never spoken of it, but since Mama died, I have sorely missed the presence of an older and wiser woman in my life."

For an instant Cressida thought she had blundered, for her godmother's face crumpled.

"Oh, pray do not distress yourself," she rushed to

kneel beside her chair. "I would not have you upset for all the world."

"I am not . . . you can have no idea how dearly I longed for a child, but it was not to be. And now you are here—Arabella's daughter, and I feel myself truly blessed. So I must do right by you . . ." There was a hint of panic in her voice. "It is what your mama would have wanted—what my dear Percy would have wanted. I have been cowardly for far too long, and I cannot . . . will not let you down, now!"

Cressida knew she must choose her words carefully. "Of course you won't, for I have all kinds of things planned. But only when you are ready. First, you must learn to resist Miss Cheam's foolish megrims. There is nothing wrong with you that a change of scene and a little fresh air cannot put right."

"But can we be sure? It is my nerves, you see . . . the crowds . . . Dr. Grantly fears that any overexcitement would be most injurious . . ."

And he has made a pretty penny out of turning you into an invalid, Cressida thought, but wisely kept her own counsel.

"I thought, perhaps," Cressida murmured persuasively, "that if we were to go for a short drive—to the park, perhaps. I'm sure his lordship would provide us with a suitable carriage. And we could choose a quiet time, when there is hardly anyone about . . . then you could see how you feel. And if you still cannot face the thought of meeting people, we will work something out."

Chapter Five

The sun was shining as the carriage, brought 'round that afternoon by one of Lord Langley's coachmen, made its way along Conduit Street and stopped outside the salon of Madame Fanchon.

Cressida turned to her godmother, searching her plump features for signs of panic. It had been a slow painstaking progression from discreet forays into the park in a closed carriage at an hour guaranteed to be thought unfashionable, to the occasional drive down Bond Street. As the weather became warmer she had consented to drive in a barouche with the hood down. And now, for the first time, Lady Kilbride had consented to leave the safe haven of the carriage.

"I am quite ready, my dear," her ladyship declared in answer to Cressida's gentle enquiry, only a slight tremor in her voice betraying her nervousness as she was helped down.

"I promise you will not be disappointed, dear ma'am," Cressida assured her, taking her arm and leading her across the pavement to the showrooms of the most renowned of London's modistes. This was not Cressida's first visit. She had earlier visited the salon to confirm that it was all Mr. Devenham had promised. And she had not been disappointed. The tastefully decorated room with its alcoves, discreetly curtained, and the little gilded chairs and long mirrors gave exactly the right atmosphere of privacy and elegance without ostentation.

As Madame Fanchon, slim and fluid of figure, came forward graciously to greet them, Lady Kilbride drew an unsteady breath and for a moment Cressida wondered if she was doing the right thing, or whether it would all be too much for her godmother. But the shrewd Madame, who had been forewarned by Cressida, knew exactly how to set her ladyship at ease, and in no time at all had her seated in the most comfortable chair and was coaxing her into considering the rival merits of silver-grey taffety and a twilled silk in deepest purple. Would her ladyship, she wondered, consider a soft brown wool that would make a charming pelisse?

"Oh, dear . . . I'm not sure . . ." Lady Kilbride murmured as Madame begged her to face the mirror and permit that she should hold it against her. At that moment she experienced the strangest of feelings, for whilst a part of her longed to cling to the safety of her blacks, a sudden stirring of something that was akin to pleasure took her by surprise, bringing a tinge of color to her cheeks. For surely Madame was right— the brown did have a softer, kinder look than her blacks, making her look quite different—and, dare she think it, a little younger?

"Oh, do have it, dear ma'am," Cressida exclaimed. "It is most becoming. The others, too. That grey taffety exactly matches your eyes."

Lady Kibride still demurred, but the feeling came again, and deep inside her other sensations that she had thought quite dead began to stir. It was as though she had suddenly been released from a spell, and more than that—as her eyes misted, she had the curious notion that Percy was there, nodding and smiling his consent. The illusion lasted but a moment, but the emotions aroused by the experience were such as she had not experienced in years, and in consequence she became quite animated.

"Yes, indeed. I will have them all," she declared.

"And there was a very pretty mauve silk you showed me. I will have that also."

Cressida gazed at her in astonishment. Never in her wildest imaginings had she hoped for such a turnabout.

"And now it is your turn, my dear," Lady Kilbride insisted.

"For the young mademoiselle, all things are possible," Madame exclaimed, by now assured of a handsome return for her labors. "Nothing too *jeune fille*. Rather it must be very simple, but also elegant. *Mousseline de soie* over a slip of pale gold, I think, for evening. And to the ankle, only. A friend, a Parisian, has managed to send me some of the latest fashion plates—life goes on as ever there, in spite of all—and this is the very latest style—a simple bell shape, and you have the figure to carry it—also an air of confidence that is seldom to be observed in the *debutante*. As for the rest, we may be a little daring, I think."

She brought forth such an array of beautiful materials—crepes, twilled silks, *mousseline de soie,* that Cressida hardly knew where to begin. "And also for you, because the color will become you, I will make a Chinese robe of rose pink silk, exquisitely embroidered, which will be very much *de rigueur*. And a braided pelisse in a color of your choosing."

Cressida left Madame's salon in a kind of daze. She had expected to have to coax and cajole Lady Kilbride into shedding her gloomy blacks. But the whole afternoon had been turned on its head in a fashion little short of spectacular.

"You will not believe it, my lord," she confided, when he arrived late in the day, just as she was coming down the stairs. She drew him aside, the words tumbling out as she related all that had happened. "I could scarce believe it myself. It was not simply a matter of dresses and the like. As we were leaving the salon, Lady Kilbride actually asked Madame if she could recommend a good hairdresser. Oh, and Miss Cheam has given notice. That is perhaps the best news of all. She is to go and live with a cousin in Brighton."

"It would seem you have been busy to some purpose," he murmured as she paused for breath.

Something in his voice made Cressida pause and search his face. It had that closed look she was coming to know. Until that moment she hadn't realized how much she had been looking forward to telling him of her small triumphs, to receiving his approbation. Now, like a bubble pricked, her elation drained away.

"I have done nothing, my lord. At least, nothing that would make me in the least ashamed, and I have certainly made no attempt to coerce your aunt. After she had got over her initial nerves she was like a new woman—if you had been there you would have been amazed." His expression did not change, and in a moment of pique she added, "But perhaps you would prefer that Lady Kilbride remained a recluse."

"Don't be ridiculous."

His curtness fuelled her resentment, driving her to blurt out, without stopping to think, "Or maybe you are simply jealous that I have succeeded where you failed."

It was as if she had touched a raw nerve. His eyes narrowed to hard, frightening slits. "You go too far, young lady. Five minutes here and you think you can work miracles. But have a care. Things aren't always that simple. I assure you that nothing would please me more than to see Aunt Beatrice restored to her former self, as long as she is not rushed into something she is unable to sustain."

"Lady Kibride has been very good to me," Cressida protested, chin up. "I would never do anything to cause her harm."

"Not deliberately, perhaps. But, have a care. Your impetuosity could well be in danger of carrying you away. All is fine for now, but as to the long-term effects, only time will tell."

She felt like a rebuked child. And as always, when rebuked, she became stubborn. "It will indeed. Since you are determined to be censorious, I may as well tell you that your aunt also means to have her reception rooms fully refurbished—and that suggestion did not come from me, though I think it an excellent idea, for in my opinion one's surroundings are almost as important as the clothes one wears, and she has been far too long in that dreary room."

Her eyes challenged him to deny it, but after an uncomfortable moment of silence, he inclined his head. "So be it. There seems little point in arguing about something that is a *fait accompli*."

But she knew that would not be the end of it. And that if anything went wrong, the blame would be laid at her door.

There was little time to brood, however, for word soon spread, aided by the few stalwart ladies who had remained in contact with Lady Kilbride, that following upon the arrival of her godchild, her house in Mount Street was to be refurbished, and she would soon be receiving once more.

Of these few, none was more delighted than Mrs. Arlington, who, though several years younger, was probably her ladyship's closest friend, and had tried many times without success to tempt her back into the real world.

Matilda Arlington had been out of town when Cressida arrived, but on her return lost no time in paying her dear friend a visit, curious to see for herself whether the rumors she had heard were true.

"My dear, you have already worked wonders!" she exclaimed, upon entering the salon where Lady Kilbride had for so long spent her days, to find that the depressing wall covering was already gone, to be replaced by a pale-green-and-cream stripe. There were cheerful rugs scattered across the floor and in place of the gloomy curtains, soft green-velvet ones were caught back with tasselled swags. "And as for your looks!" she exclaimed with the privilege of an old friend. "I have not seen you so elegant in years!"

Lady Kilbride blushed with pleasure. "Oh, this is nothing. We have hardly begun. It is like a miracle, Tilly. And I have my dear godchild, Cressida, to thank for everything. She is so like her mother, not perhaps in looks, but in her sweet nature, though her self-confidence and determination come from her father. I am sorry she is not here at present, for I should very much like you to meet her."

"There will be time enough for that." She drew her chair closer. "For now, do tell me everything about her."

As the words tumbled out of Lady Kilbride, Tilly found her memory straying back through the years, when everyone, herself included, had watched with envy as the catch of the Season, Charles Merriton, had assiduously courted the young and very vulnerable Beatrice Warley. Small wonder that she had fallen head over ears in love with him. She had been a pretty girl, Tilly remembered, and perhaps, if Arabella had not come along with her heart-stopping loveliness and sweet nature . . . Arabella, who had been Bea's best friend. But Fate had not been kind. For Charles had taken one look—and the rest was history.

Eventually, of course, Lord Kilbride had come on the scene. He was older and prodigiously wealthy, and one could not doubt that he had cherished Beatrice. It had been a model marriage—and perhaps, if he had been able to give her children—but then, "perhaps" seldom held much sway in real life.

"Cressida is a dear girl."

Tilly collected her thoughts as Beatrice continued,

"She has such an agreeable and indeed persuasive way with her that one finds it quite impossible to resist."

"Which is exactly what you need, my dear. It is more than time that you began to live again. Which reminds me, I am having a small at-home next Wednesday. Several people you may know. Do come and bring Cressida with you. My Celia is a little younger, but they will surely get on."

A wave of relief flooded Lady Kilbride. "That would be splendid, Tilly. A friend nearer her own age is exactly what she needs. For, although I am much improved, and much as I cherish her, there are times when I find Cressida's sheer energy a trifle overwhelming, and I daresay she finds me tiresomely slow. In fact—and I have said this to no one—I had been dreading the prospect of hosting her come-out, with all that it would entail. But she insists that it is quite unnecessary, and that if her father wishes to present her at court, he may do so in his own good time. So dear Alastair is to give a ball in her honor at Grosvenor Square so that she may become acquainted with everyone."

"Well, there you are. All you will have to do is enjoy the event. And my little soiree will help to ease you into being in company once more."

Lord Langley was less sanguine about Mrs. Arlington's invitation, as Cressida found when they met later the following afternoon. He was just leaving after his customary visit and she was coming downstairs.

"Aunt Beatrice tells me you are to accompany her to one of Matilda Arlington's affairs. Do you think that is wise?"

She paused on the last stair so that she might face him eye to eye. His expression was unreadable. "Do I take it that you don't approve?"

"I haven't said so. Though I do have reservations about her being rushed into change. Driving in the park is one thing—being trapped in a crowded room in a strange house is quite another."

"I would hardly call Mrs. Arlington's house strange, my lord. They are old friends, are they not? So my godmother must have been there many times in the past, and will most likely know some of the other guests."

"Even so . . ."

"In any case, whatever you may choose to think, it is for your aunt to decide. She is not senile, nor is she a coward. I believe she just needs a little encouragement. And this may be the least stressful way to ease her back into society."

His eyes narrowed as he watched the determined set of Cressida's chin. "In other words, you have made up your mind."

"I didn't say that! It is not my decision, but I respect and admire her courage—her willingness to take the next step. Quite simply, we have made a beginning and now we have to move on." The raw passion in her voice threatened to overcome her. "And if Lady Kilbride finds herself unable to face the company of even a few people, then—we must think again." Her chin lifted. "But at least we shall have tried."

He looked at her long and hard. "So be it," he said, inclined his head, and took his leave of her.

It was as well that Lord Langley was not with them, for when the time came, the sound of so many voices all speaking at once very nearly made Lady Kilbride turn tail and flee back to her waiting carriage. Her mouth dried, and just for a moment everything seemed to be closing in on her. Only Cressida's hand comfortingly firm beneath her arm, sustained her, and her "It will be all right, dear ma'am, I promise you" prevented her from such a display of cowardice.

The blurring of her ladyship's eyes cleared. "Yes . . .

yes, of course. It's just . . . I had not expected so many . . . how very foolish you must think me."

"Indeed I don't. I think you are being very courageous. Mrs. Arlington will know that you don't wish to stay long. And James is to remain here with the carriage so that you may return home as soon as you wish."

"Yes—yes, of course. Take no notice of my foolishness. You are sure I look all right?"

Cressida glanced at the pretty mauve silk gown beneath her godmother's woollen wrap, and the matching lace cap which graced her prematurely white hair.

"I think you look very fine," she said, gently drawing her into a large cool hallway fragrant with flowers, where they were met by Mrs. Arlington, who had been watching out for them.

"You came," she exclaimed. "I promise you won't be disappointed." She signalled to a maid to take their wraps before ushering them into a large salon, where a number of people were already gathered, several of whom were known to Lady Kilbride, though she hadn't seen them for years.

Cressida followed anxiously, as, after the initial greetings, Mrs. Arlington led them through to a large airy salon where, enveloped in a buzz of conversation, a number of ladies were already gathered. The sound faded momentarily into curiosity as her godmother was settled into a comfortable chair, and then began again as several ladies whom she hadn't met for years expressed their pleasure upon seeing her ladyship.

Cressida sighed thankfully as gradually, like someone coming out of a long, dark tunnel, her godmother began to relax and respond.

"I think," murmured Mrs. Arlington, "that she will be all right. So now let me introduce you to my dear Celia."

A lovely creature with the fairest of curls, a delicate

complexion and a sylphlike figure clad in palest blue muslin, came to her mother's side.

"You remember I told you about Cressida, dear. She is staying with Lady Kilbride."

"Yes, of course. Mama says you have come all the way from Lisbon. Were you not terrified, being so close to the war? I'm sure I would have been," she said, sounding slightly envious.

"Good gracious, no." Cressida laughed. "There was very little danger. And if I had ever succumbed to nerves, my father would long ago have disowned me."

"Goodness!" Celia exclaimed, a little in awe, but liking Cressida more every moment. "Do come along and let me introduce you to some of my friends."

How young she seemed—so young that Cressida found it difficult to believe there was only about eighteen months between them. However, she allowed herself to be drawn into a group of Celia's friends, several of whom gazed enviously at Cressida's gown of amber crepe edged at neck and hem with tiny white rosebuds, which even to their inexperienced eyes bore the hallmark of fashion.

The time passed pleasantly enough, and Cressida kept a close eye on her godmother, who seemed to be holding up quite well. Even so, when she deemed sufficient time had elapsed, she approached her with the suggestion that they might leave whenever she wished. Lady Kilbride thanked her kindly for the thought, but she had not yet spoken to old Mrs. Goodbody, who had used to be a regular visitor to Mount Street in the days when she was receiving.

"Such delightful music," she confessed sometime later as the carriage took them home. "I declare I am quite exhausted."

"But you did enjoy the afternoon?" Cressida asked anxiously, for fear it had all been too much, and she would have to endure another dressing down from Alastair.

"Oh, my dear girl, I haven't felt so alive for years, and I owe it all to you! So many old friends I met, such expressions of kindness—" Lady Kilbride sighed. "All those years wasted."

Her words brought a stupid thickness to Cressida's throat. She swallowed, and said thickly, "But so many more fulfilling ones to come, dear ma'am."

Chapter Six

Word swiftly got round that Lady Kilbride was about to come out of her self-induced seclusion. The few friends who had remained in touch with her were both surprised and delighted to learn that she would soon be receiving as she had used to do.

Meanwhile the house was still being turned inside out and painted and polished. Martha had been obliged to take on extra help, for, as she had been heard to grumble, "These old bones 'en't fit fer all these goin's-on."

Her ladyship on the other hand had discovered that there was something remarkably liberating about the whole experience. When Percy died, he had left her handsomely provided for, but of what use was money when there was no incentive to spend it—and no one to appreciate it.

And then Cressida had arrived on the scene, every inch her mother's daughter, and everything had changed. Together they had pored over patterns for wall coverings and curtains to complement the new Aubusson carpet that had been ordered. And with every passing day she could feel herself shedding the years—all those wasted years when she had shut herself away.

"I cannot tell you how glad I am that you came to me, my dear," Lady Kilbride said for the umpteenth time as they drove in the park on a sunny afternoon, her ladyship resplendent in her soft brown pelisse and a most becoming hat. Her eyes were bright, and there was a hint of color in her cheeks. "When I consider how dreary my situation had become, I wonder that I didn't molder away from sheer boredom." She turned and patted Cressida's hand. "Now, everything is changing. And I owe it all to you."

"I did very little, ma'am. You simply needed someone to voice your inner longings, a fresh pair of eyes to make you aware of all you were missing. If I was that person, then I am glad."

They were not alone in the park. In fact, Cressida was surprised at the number of people who had been coaxed out of doors by the sunshine. An air of optimism prevailed as everywhere carriages were being pulled over to allow their occupants to step down. The great frost that had frozen the River Thames and kept them indoors was now a dim and distant memory and people's spirits were high, for the war was over. Napoleon had acknowledged defeat. He had already abdicated and sailed for the isle of Elba, there to rule over his few remaining loyal subjects. And, please God, their loved ones would no longer be in danger and might soon be coming home.

"Beatrice! By all that's wonderful—it is you!" the booming voice came from a stationary landau with its hood down. A hat adorned with a nodding plume was thrust forward to reveal plump features that would not see fifty again.

"Gussie! Oh, what a splendid surprise! Henry, pray stop the carriage."

"Scarcely recognized you," the voice continued. "Surprised to see you, in fact. Heard you had retired from the world and here you are, looking ten years younger."

Lady Kilbride beamed with pleasure. "I feel ten years younger"—she reached out a hand to Cressida—"and it is all due to my dear godchild. You will re-

member Arabella Merriton—Arabella Fairburn that
was, who was my dearest friend . . ."

"Of course I remember her. Married Charles Merriton—you were sweet on him at the time, as I recall.
Thought y'r heart was broken."

Her ladyship's cheeks grew hot, aware that Cressida
was looking at her with lively curiosity. Her heart
lurched and she didn't know where to look. "Oh,
that . . . a young girl's crush, Gussie—nothing more."
She managed a depreciating laugh and attempted to
give Augusta's thoughts a new direction. "Allow me
to make Arabella's daughter known to you. She is
staying with me for the Season. Cressida, my dear, this
is Lady Augusta Merton, a friend of many years
standing."

"I am very pleased to meet you, ma'am," Cressida
said, not daring to look at her godmother for fear
she would betray her curiosity about Lady Augusta's
revealing comments concerning her and Papa.

"And I, you, m'dear. I like to see pretty manners
in a young girl," Lady Augusta boomed, quite unaware of her gaffe. The plume nodded vigorously as
she raised her lorgnette. "You have something of y'r
mother about the eyes, though you ain't as pretty.
Beauty of her day was Arabella. You are much more
y'r father's daughter."

"Gussie!" Lady Kilbride was mortified by such out-
spokeness, but Cressida only laughed and declared
herself well satisfied to be thought so.

And that was how the earl saw her as he turned to
greet a group of friends. There was an uninhibited
springtime freshness in her laughter that was wanting
in many of her contemporaries. He excused himself
and walked across to where the two carriages stood
abreast of one another. "Ladies," he said, tipping his
hat to each in turn.

"Good to see you out, Aunt Bea. And looking very

fine, if I may say so. You have chosen a good day to take the air."

"But a shade fresh for standing about," said Lady Augusta. She poked her coachman with a gold-handled cane. "So I'll bid you good day. I am holding a small soiree on Friday evening, Beatrice. Nothing fancy—a little music, some conversation—you know the kind of thing—you'll be very welcome if you'd care for it. Daresay you might meet some old friends. Bring Miss Merriton if you wish. Cavannah's girls will be there amongst others. As for you, Langley—come if you've a fancy to, though you'd find it tame fare, I daresay. Up to you." The coachman received another prod. "Drive on, Jasper."

"What a strange, formidable lady," Cressida murmured, as the carriage disappeared from view.

"Indeed," said his lordship dryly. "Quite a character is Lady Augusta. I've even seen her silence Lady Jersey, and that takes some doing."

"She was ever an oddity," Lady Kilbride agreed. "But there is a very generous spirit beneath that brusque manner, though she would not have it said. She is acknowledged to be one of the wealthiest women in England, and is a great patroness of the arts. However, that is neither here nor there." She turned to her nephew. "Alastair, perhaps if you are not otherwise committed, you might care to introduce Cressida to some of your friends."

"There really is no need, ma'am." Cressida, remembering their last encounter, did not need to await his reaction. "I'm sure his lordship has better things to do than bear-lead me, and besides, I came out to keep you company."

"Which you have done quite admirably—and I am not ungrateful, for you have wrought wonders. But I must not be selfish. The sooner you become acquainted with people nearer your own age, the happier I shall be." She fixed the earl with a look that dared him to refuse.

"Then so be it." One eyebrow lifted quizzically. "Miss Merriton?" He extended a hand to help her down. And as she still held back, said "You had much better give in gracefully. I long ago discovered that it is pointless to argue with my aunt once she has made up her mind. Besides, she has a point. It is high time you began to widen your circle of acquaintances."

"Exactly," said her ladyship. "Henry shall tool me around the park and then take me home. Alastair can bring you back to Mount Street when you are ready."

Cressida had no choice but to agree, though she disliked being forced into accepting a decision that was not of her making. They crossed the park in silence until the earl said dryly, "I do hope you are not going to sulk all afternoon."

"I never sulk!" she exclaimed.

"Then allow me to tell you that you are at this moment giving an excellent impression of doing so."

"I simply dislike the idea of being foisted upon you."

"Then I suggest you disabuse yourself of any such notion. For, whatever you may care to believe, I am not my aunt's lackey, engaged to do her bidding. Furthermore, I never do anything I don't wish to do."

By now she was woefully aware of behaving in a manner that verged on childishness, without knowing quite how to extricate herself. But in the end it was he who extricated her.

"However, there is one thing I must set straight." His hand beneath her arm brought them to a halt, and he turned her to face him. "At our last meeting I was less than appreciative of the miracle you seem to have worked with Aunt Beatrice. It seems you were right and I was wrong, and I wish you to know that I am grateful to see her so changed."

She hardly knew what to say. It must have cost him

dear to offer her an apology. In the end she was saved from her dilemma by the arrival of Mr. Devenham, and only had time to murmur, "Thank you. I had hoped—but she has surprised even me."

"Miss Merriton, what a pleasant surprise," Mr. Devenham murmured, making an elegant leg. "And looking quite delightful, if I may say so without appearing odiously presumptuous. Makes the whole afternoon worthwhile."

She smiled at this absurdity, for it was quite impossible to take him seriously. The hint of an answering smile lurking in his eyes suggested that he knew exactly what she was thinking and totally agreed with her.

"I believe you have already wrought wonders with her ladyship, Miss Merriton. Alastair tells me she is a changed lady."

"A change for the better, I hope. I did have a few qualms of conscience, for fear of driving her into even deeper gloom. But I could not bear to see her so diminished, and decided that to at least try to coax her out of it was better than doing nothing."

"Very astute, ma'am." Mr. Devenham raised his quizzing glass. "I see you also decided to avail yourself of Madame Fanchon's good offices—and to excellent effect."

"Thank you. It is kind of you to notice."

"Couldn't help but notice. That shade of green mirrors your eyes almost exactly."

"To be honest, I thoroughly enjoyed myself. It was quite wonderful to watch Madame coaxing my godmother out of her excess of nerves. By the end, Lady Kilbride had become positively animated, Madame's order book was overflowing, and I now find myself in possession of more dresses than I can possibly wear."

Mr. Devenham smiled his sleepy smile. "But only consider the pleasure you will render to gentlemen such as myself as we sigh over each new creation."

Cressida tried and failed to look shocked. "Now you are being absurd, sir."

"Perhaps—just a little."

"Perry tipping the butter boat again, is he?" Alastair, having left them for a few minutes, had returned with a vision of loveliness clinging to his arm, silver-fair curls fluttering against a blue bonnet, her curvaceous figure showing to advantage beneath the flimsiest of muslin skirts, topped by a close-fitting little velvet jacket of a blue that exactly matched her lovely eyes.

"Not quite up to Madame Fanchon's style, I fear," Mr. Devenham had murmured as they approached. "But love is blind, so they say."

Was this then the earl's current *chère amie*? Cressida wondered, surprised—even a trifle disappointed—that he should aspire to anyone quite so—obvious?

"I am very pleased to meet you, Miss Merriton," the vision murmured in an attractive husky voice as they were introduced. "Alastair has told me all about you."

Did the earl look disconcerted? Cressida dearly hoped so, for she knew how he despised gossips. But the look was gone in a minute. And the young lady seemed too besotted to be aware of anyone or anything but herself. Cressida did not care to be talked about in such a way, yet the temptation to pursue the conversation was irresistible.

"Has he, indeed? Then you clearly have the advantage of me, Miss Devine, for he has told me nothing about you."

It was not meant as a compliment, but for some reason, she seemed to take it as one. "I think you are incredibly brave to have travelled so far alone," she confessed with a tiny shudder, and managing somehow to make it sound as though Cressida in some way lacked her sensitivity. "Indeed, I am sure I should have been quite petrified at the mere thought of being tossed in rough seas, to say nothing of being a woman alone with all those coarse sailors . . ."

The young woman's prurience was insupportable. As was his lordship's outrageous presumption in discussing her with this pert miss. "I fear his lordship must have given you quite the wrong impression." Cressida's tone was light, but it contained a hint of steel. "Far from being reliant upon the ship's crew to bear me company, gallant though they were, I was supported throughout the voyage by some dear friends. In fact, the nearest I came to being alone was when his lordship and I put up for the night at an inn on our way to London."

It was infamous of her even to hint at any suggestion of impropriety, but the temptation to shock was irresistible. And just for a moment she saw the young woman's eyes widen, her complacency waver, which made the risk worthwhile, whatever the consequences.

There followed a moment of complete silence when she dared not look at the earl's face.

It was Mr. Devenham who broke it by saying in his droll way, "How very brave of you. I make it a practice never to sleep away from home, for how can one be absolutely certain that the sheets have been aired."

"Very wise, Perry," said the earl. It was impossible to read anything into the brief comment, but his profile was less than encouraging. Cressida was just wondering how best to extricate herself when she was hailed by a familiar and totally unexpected voice.

"Miss Merriton—can it really be you?"

A familiar figure came striding toward her across the green sward.

Count Henri von Schroder was decidedly handsome in a rather flamboyant fashion, effusive and very sure of himself. There had been rumors of his amors— some less savory than others. Their paths had crossed many times in Lisbon, and he had shown a decided interest in her, enhanced perhaps by her reluctance to succumb to his flattery. Although no more than four-and-twenty, he was already a trifle fleshy and in time would run to fat, but for now he looked the perfect picture of a very royal personage, as indeed he was, being closely related to at least two Austrian grand dukes.

"I had not expected to see you here, Count."

"It was a surprise for me, also." Dark eyes gleamed beneath black brows as he raised the hand she extended to his lips.

One could not fault his behavior, and there was no doubting his charm, but she had always found something rather predatory about him. Also it irked her that she knew him to be something of a turncoat, for it was well-known in Lisbon that when Austria had allied itself with Bonaparte, the count had been one of his most enthusiastic supporters. Now, she concluded, that allegiance was conveniently forgotten.

"However," he continued, "it would seem that, with hostilities all but at an end, London is to be the venue for the celebration of the peace. And one must participate. I am at the Pulteney in Piccadilly. Do you know it?"

"By reputation only, sir. I am staying with my aunt in Mount Street."

"I understand that festivities are already being planned, and that your Prince Regent is preparing apartments at St. James's Palace for the Russian emperor."

"A little premature, surely," murmured Mr. Devenham. "The czar may have other plans."

The irony of this comment escaped the count. "I think not. It seems to me entirely fitting."

There was a moment of silence, and Cressida seized the opportunity to introduce the count to her companions, very much aware of Lord Langley's glance following her as she did so. Count von Schroder greeted each of them with the same degree of amiability, but

Cressida was not surprised to observe how often his glance strayed to the delectable Miss Devine. She was exactly the kind of woman he would find both irresistible and willing. She saw that his interest had not escaped the earl's notice, though only a slight thinning of the lips betrayed his displeasure.

"Have you received news of your father recently?" von Schroder enquired of Cressida.

"Not a word. But, you know Pa—he will be far too engrossed in his current exploits to worry about me."

"Then he should worry." His prominent nose flared with sudden hauteur. "In Guerdenstatt we guard our womenfolk more carefully."

"So I have heard, sir. I can only praise the Lord that I am English and have a liberal-minded father."

"Oh, but only consider how wonderful it must feel to be so cherished," Miss Devine exclaimed and sighed at the thought. She moved a fraction closer to the handsome Austrian, gazing up at him, wide-eyed.

The earl's expression remained inscrutable.

"I have no wish to consider any such thing," Cressida retorted. "It wouldn't suit me at all to be so closely confined."

For a moment the count's handsome brow darkened. "Yet one must consider the dangers, the temptations—Lord Langley will surely agree with me that young ladies such as yourself must always be protected?"

"I beg you won't drag me into the argument, sir," the earl returned with feeling. "I am not Miss Merriton's keeper, thank God. That daunting obligation falls to my aunt, which is probably just as well for I would not relish the task. Were I involved, we should be forever at odds."

"Oh, how unfair! I am, in general, the most conciliating of creatures. Is that not so, Mr. Devenham?"

He smiled gently at her. "From our brief acquaintance I have certainly found you to be everything that one would wish you to be."

The count shrugged, his good humor returning. "That is a compliment, indeed. So for you, my dear Miss Merriton, we shall make an exception." His predatory glance strayed once more to Isabella Devine, and Cressida wondered how long it would be before he attempted to wrest the "divine Devine" away from the earl.

Chapter Seven

The whole country rejoiced in the sunshine, and London was gripped by celebration fever. The streets were thronged with excited onlookers as all the foreign dignitaries began to arrive, providing a feast for the eyes and joy to the gossips. Early arrivals had been King Frederick of Prussia and the handsome young emperor of Russia, Czar Alexander—the latter, so it was rumored, having infuriated the Prince of Wales by declining the state apartments prepared for him at St. James's, preferring instead to join his sister, the Grand Duchess Catherine of Oldenburg at the Pulteney Hotel.

"Prinny is rumored to be beside himself with rage," murmured Mr. Devenham, who was attending a soiree with a small group of friends, most of whom were known to Cressida with the exception of a young Guards officer, Major Harry Pelham, whose pallor and an empty sleeve revealed him to have been wounded in battle. "Can't blame him, of course. Shabby behavior, when all's said and done. And made worse when the czar declined to attend a dinner at Carlton House. The sister's doing, I shouldn't wonder. Formidable woman. Poor fellow's said to be very much under her thumb. Still, it's all highly entertaining."

Cressida had little time for gossip, but she could hardly fail to be amused by Perry's gentle barbs. "You seem to know a great deal about all that goes on."

His eyebrow quirked comically. "Oh, well—you

know how it is, I seem to have the kind of face that makes people long to confide in me. And everyone knows that I am quite harmless, after all."

She laughed. "Of course. Is it true that the cows in Green Park have been frightened by all the cheering and are refusing to give milk?"

He shuddered gently. "Now, there you have me. I know nothing about cows, nor do I wish to learn."

"For shame!"

"I admit it is a failing in me, but then, no one is perfect. Perhaps Harry can enlighten you."

"Major Pelham?"

A faint blush relieved his pallor. "Sorry, Miss Merriton. Anything to do with horses, and I'm your man, but cows . . ." He blushed, clearly embarrassed.

"Ah, well, no matter." To give his mind a new direction, she changed the subject, saying lightly, "I wouldn't be surprised if it were true, though. For, as if the cheering weren't enough, I am reliably informed that there is an enormous edifice being built within the park with much noise and upset—an inspiration of the Prince Regent, so they say—to be known as the Castle of Discord. And at the beginning of August, with the aid of rockets and fireworks, there is to be a realistic reproduction of the siege of Bajados after which a small army of workmen will perform a miracle by turning it into a Temple of Concord."

"Would that matters could have been that simple," Major Pelham said with quiet bitterness. "I lost two of my best friends there."

"Oh, no, I am so sorry, Major!" Cressida felt the tears come into her throat. How could she have been so insensitive? "Forgive me—I just didn't stop to think."

He was quick to absolve her. "Why should you, my dear Miss Merriton? It was but a momentary reminder of things best forgotten. Truly, I w-would not have you upset for all the world."

"Thank you. You are kinder than I deserve."

She could almost feel the earl's displeasure as a physical barb, but could not bring herself to meet his eyes.

"Lady Kilbride seems to be enjoying life to the full once more," observed Mr. Devenham, coming to her rescue. She turned to him with gratitude.

"Oh, I do hope so. There were moments when I wondered if I was just being selfish," she said jerkily. "But now she is getting about and meeting people, she really does seem much happier." Her voice faltered and she drew a deep breath. "I am aware it is a failing in me that sometimes my enthusiasm carries me away. I don't mean to ride roughshod over people's feelings, but . . ."

"You must not refine upon his reaction just now, you know," he said quietly. "Harry ain't a man to take things wrong or bear grudges."

"No." She blinked away the tears that stung her eyes and tried to smile. "Even so, after all I have seen and experienced, I simply cannot believe that I spoke with such a want of sensitivity."

"He knows that well enough, m'dear. We all, I hope, already know you too well to suppose you capable of any such thing."

"You are very generous. However, I think Lord Langley will be less easy to convince. My crassness merely confirms what he already believes—that I am light-minded and much too coming for his liking."

"Alastair has never given me any such impression. And I believe I know him well enough to detect his likes and dislikes."

She was not so sure. However it was not in her nature to brood, and as she made new friends and more and more invitations began to proliferate on the mantleshelf, life took on a faster pace, and her godmother's talk became almost wholly concerned with the forthcoming ball.

"I suppose we must visit Grosvenor Square very soon. You will wish to see for yourself what arrangements need to be made, although Alastair will take care of most things."

"Always supposing he is still agreeable."

"Well, of course he will be agreeable. Why should he not be? It is all arranged."

It was on the tip of Cressida's tongue to confess that she and her ladyship's nephew were, if not exactly at daggers drawn, certainly less than best of friends. And, being unsure quite how to put matters right, she had recently been at great pains not to be present when the earl visited his aunt, and he had been scrupulously polite whenever they met elsewhere. And yet it had not always been so. There had been moments when they had dealt quite agreeably together. That the present situation was partly of her making certainly weighed on her conscience. Pa had taught her always to face problems squarely, and she supposed the earl must certainly constitute a problem, so a way would have to be found to set things right.

Her mind made up, Cressida waited until her aunt had gone to rest as usual after they had enjoyed a light nuncheon, before dressing with particular care in a new pelisse of soft green velvet that echoed her eyes, buttoned high at the neck, and skimming the swell of breast and hip. A neat bonnet in the same velvet framed her face. Jane Batty had gone to Pimlico to visit a sick aunt, so she asked Martha if she might borrow Meg for an hour or so to accompany her on a visit. The housekeeper was consumed with curiosity, but dutifully summoned the child, bade her put on her best coat and hat—and to be sure to be good and mind her manners.

It was not the first time she had seen Langley House, but until now, it had only been from the confines of her godmother's carriage. Now, standing before its imposing gates, and looking up at the windows glinting back at her in the sunlight, she felt the first stirrings of unease.

"Are we goin' in 'ere, miss?" the awed maid whispered.

Cressida straightened her shoulders. "Yes, of course."

"Cor!"

Cor, indeed, she echoed silently, suddenly aware of what she was about to do. And immediately reproached herself for cowardice.

But the imposing front was as nothing to the interior when they were admitted by a liveried porter who eyed Cressida with deep suspicion as she stated her business, and asked her to wait while he summoned the majordomo.

She had been entertained in many grand houses in Lisbon, but none as fine as this. She turned slowly, taking in the cool classical expanse of marble-lozenged floors; of fine Corinthian columns that carried the eye upward to a ceiling exquisitely panelled and painted.

"Do you approve?"

Lord Langley's voice, dry as ever, brought her down to earth with a start. He had paused halfway down the staircase, which rose, curving with all the delicate grace of a swan's neck, to the landing above, one hand lightly resting on its delicate wrought-iron rail. And she was immediately embarrassed, as though she had been caught prying.

"How could one not approve?" she said at last. "I have never seen anything quite so perfect. Lisbon has many beautiful houses, but by comparison, they are overelaborate."

"The ceiling is reckoned to be one of James Wyatt's finest."

She lifted her head again to trace the artistry of each panel—and Langley found himself admiring the purity of her profile beneath her bonnet, and was in no hurry to end the moment.

"Oh, forgive me," she said, suddenly aware of the prolonged silence. "You must think me quite ill-mannered."

"Not at all," he murmured, and held out a hand. "You had better come and see a little of the rest."

"Oh. But are you not busy? I came only to settle a time when we might discuss arrangements for the ball. Your aunt is beginning to fret a little."

"Now is as good a time as any. John, take the child to the kitchen. I'm sure Cook will manage to find her a cake or two."

The drawing room proved to be as beautiful in its way as the hall, with another wonderful ceiling, walls lined with turquoise silk, and rows of tall windows on two sides, from one side of which one could look across to Hyde Park. "Quite perfect," she said, turning away at last.

"My mother would have been be pleased to hear you say so. It was ever her favorite room. Come and sit down," he said, indicating one of several sofas scattered across the room. The ivory plush velvet received her with cushioned ease, as her feet sank into a luxurious pale gold carpet.

Cressida was not aware of his summoning a servant, but as if by magic one arrived almost immediately carrying a loaded tray, which he set down on the table before them. "Gracious!" she exclaimed. "I have never seen so many delicious cakes!"

"Cook's specials, they are, madam—and she hopes as you'll enjoy them." The young man's face broke into a grin. "Your little maid's havin' a right good tuck in."

Cressida laughed. "I must warn her not to over-praise them to our cook, or she may give notice."

"Yes, madam." He blushed, suddenly conscious of the earl's eye on him and the gross impropriety of speaking so familiarly to one of his master's guests. He bowed and hurriedly withdrew.

The earl had watched the exchange with some interest. It would seem that his aunt's protégée was equally at home with princes and servants, which could not be said of many young women of his acquaintance. He watched her now presiding with equal ease over teacups so fine, they seemed almost transparent.

"Your servants are well trained," she said. "I am impressed. But then, I rather think I was meant to be."

"Touché." For once his smile lacked any hint of cynicism. He indicated a bell concealed beneath the mantelpiece. "It has its uses. For tea I ring once. If I have a less-than-welcome guest, I ring twice, and John will enter almost immediately to remind me that I have an urgent appointment."

"For shame, sir!"

"Not at all. The bore must try again another day. No one is hurt, and I am spared the tedium of being polite."

She ought to have been shocked, but found herself laughing instead. It was clear that he had meant her to be mistress of the precious teacups, and she was not one to resist a challenge. "I had not taken you for a tea man," she said.

"Nor am I in general."

"But you were curious to see how I acquitted myself?"

He looked momentarily disconcerted—and then amused. "Do you also read minds?"

"Only occasionally. When I was first in Lisbon, it frustrated me that I didn't understand the language. And as a child at an awkward age, with a mother who was frequently unwell, I was often left to my own devices. So I used to watch and listen. It is amazing how quickly you can learn."

He had this sudden picture of a lonely child set down among foreigners. Many would have become introverted, but she had shown amazing maturity.

"And after Mama died, as I probably told you, I grew up very quickly."

"And now?"

"Now I am thoroughly enjoying myself, making many new friends—though the girls are mostly younger than me and oh, so naive. I am in danger of feeling staid."

He laughed aloud, and for once there was no mockery in his laughter. "Never! We shall have to make this ball something special for you, or you may fall into a despair." He watched her cheeks turn pink. "Some very special guests, perhaps. I believe Wellington is expected very soon, and with any luck your father could be with him."

"Do you really think so? That would be wonderful, of course," she added, tempering her enthusiasm with good common sense. "Though I fear he is just as likely to remain in Paris, pursuing some pretty little barque of frailty."

He lifted a laconic eyebrow. "What a very unfilial remark. However, your fears must be unjustified in this instance, I think. Prinny is proposing to host a celebration to end all celebrations at Carlton House to which your father must surely be invited. There is also talk of valor being rewarded."

"For Wellington, of course, but Papa—I don't know." Cressida gathered up her gloves and reticule, suddenly aware that she might be outstaying her welcome. "Thank you for the tea, my lord. I fear I have taken up a good deal of your time."

"Not at all," he said smoothly, and found he meant it. "Besides, you will surely wish to see the ballroom before you leave."

"If it is no trouble . . ."

He held out a hand to draw her to her feet. "I really think you should. It is on the other side of the house. We'll take the long gallery."

This proved to be yet another experience, for the

gallery seemed to stretch forever, with many windows looking out over the gardens, and little sofas and chairs grouped at intervals. At the far end was placed a dainty spinet.

"Oh, how lovely. Do you play?"

The earl gave her a look. "Not I. My mother used to—and the occasional guest. But you will surely be proficient?"

"Oh, I have not touched a keyboard for an age. I am quite out of practice."

"Coward," he said softly.

Aware that she was being challenged, and with a small frisson of excitement and nerves, she rose to the bait. "Very well. But you have been warned, so you will be well served if I make a mull of it."

She set aside her gloves and reticule and crossed to take her seat, flexing her fingers, very conscious of his presence and wishing she had not risen to the challenge. It had been in her mind to play a brief conventional waltz, but in the very act of beginning, she looked up and saw him perched on the edge of a table, arms folded, and wearing his most ironic look. Without stopping to think, she launched into a spirited rendition of a short and extremely idiomatic French song. As she stuck the last chord, and stood up, he clapped, his irony turned to genuine amusement.

"Your versatility continues to amaze. But where did the well-bred Miss Merriton learn such unladylike ditties?"

She laughed. "Oh, you would be surprised what one may pick up among the rude soldiery, my lord."

"For shame. Now—shall we proceed? But before we do, there is something I have been meaning to say. I really think it is time you stopped 'my lording' me and called me Alastair."

She looked surprised—then smiled. "Very well. I will do so if you will stop calling me Miss Merriton in that top-lofty way."

"Agreed."

They walked on down a short pair of stairs, and he threw open the door facing them. The ballroom, though impressively large, was, by comparison with the rest of the house, a disappointment. The chandeliers were wrapped in covers, and the wall lights gave very little indication of its atmosphere. But she had experience enough to know how very different it would be, once transformed.

"If you will furnish me with a list of the people you and Aunt Beatrice wish to invite, my secretary will draw up a list and send out the invitations. We can accommodate five hundred quite comfortably."

"Good gracious! I doubt I know five hundred people," Cressida exclaimed. "I had no idea . . ."

"Aunt Beatrice will have no difficulty in finding them. And there will, of course be dinner beforehand for family and friends." He was silent for a moment. Then, "It is true that we don't always agree. That is often so, I believe, when two headstrong people are involved. But, believe me, I continue to be deeply appreciative of the transformation you have brought about in Aunt Beatrice. Let us agree that this is my way of showing it."

Chapter Eight

It was August and London had still not tired of celebrating. The month had begun with the magnificent *pièce de resistance* in Green Park, which everyone had been impatient to see, contrived for the Regent by William Congreve in which a towering Castle of Discord was dramatically transformed into a Temple of Concord. And the whole accompanied by fireworks and rockets. From then on, there were numerous displays, each hoping to outdo the other. Every hotel of note was filled to capacity; gentry who seldom left their country mansions flocked to town to join in the celebrations, hoping perhaps to be rewarded by a glimpse of the great hero, Wellington, who, it was rumored, was already in town. By day the streets and parks were crowded, some scarcely recognizable as pagodas and little oriental temples proliferated. And by night, there was many a ball, and the theatres were filled to overflowing.

"In all my days I have never known anything like it," confessed Lady Kilbride, who, having set out to drive to Green Park, had been obliged to turn back as her carriage was constantly jostled by overenthusiastic revellers. Now, having enjoyed a light nuncheon, she had repaired to the parlor with her godchild, who was for once at home. "I cannot think it at all proper for people to behave in such an abandoned fashion."

Cressida laughed. "They are just happy, dear ma'am.

I doubt many of them have much to cheer about in the ordinary way."

"I suppose there is some truth in that."

Martha put her head 'round the door. "You've got a caller, m'lady—a gentleman. Wouldn't give me 'is card. Shall I say as your not receivin' or show him in?"

Lady Kilbride glanced uncertainly at her godchild, as nerves threatened. "Oh dear, I suppose . . ." she began, but got no further as there was a disturbance at the door. It was pushed wide and a flamboyant figure filled the doorway.

"No need for cards between us, surely, Bea?"

"Pa!" Cressida exclaimed joyously, springing up from her chair to rush at him, and fling her arms about him. "Oh, Pa, why ever did you not let us know when to expect you?"

"Didn't know myself until the last minute. I say, have a care for my coat—don't want it mangled. Cost me a fortune in Paris."

He looked over Cressida's head to where Lady Kilbride sat clutching the arms of her chair.

"Beatrice! Pretty as ever, and not looking a day older, by Jove!"

Just for an instant, she was bereft of speech, turning hot, then cold as a welter of emotions raced through her. He was more portly than she remembered, his face a ruddier hue, and his hair glistening with malacca to conceal any hint of grey. But the eyes still held their wicked glint. And just for an instant she was carried back over the years, remembering that handsome, smooth-tongued young blade who, just for a short while, had made her feel like a princess. And then the mists cleared and she saw that Charles was still a handsome figure of a man—but no longer godlike. In fact, yes, she was sure that beneath his beautifully cut coat there was just the beginning of a paunch. For some reason, this discovery, combined with the fact that she was wearing one of her most becoming new gowns, had a most liberating effect upon her, so that she was able to respond to his flattery with genuine warmth.

"Nonsense, Charles. I shall not see forty again, any more than you will. But as I remember, you always were one to tip the butter boat."

He laughed aloud. "*Touché*. In the blood, y' see."

"Well, do sit down, for you quite overpower one, standing there. I believe you will find that chair to your liking." He quirked an eyebrow, but acquiesced. "And you'll take a little wine—or is brandy more to your taste?"

"No, no, I'm well enough for the moment—I can't stay long."

"We weren't sure when to expect you, Pa," Cressida said, to draw his attention away from Lady Kilbride. "Is Lord Wellington with you?"

He chuckled. "He is. And well pleased with himself. He is elevated to a dukedom, no less."

"And more than well deserved," said her ladyship. "For we all owe him so much."

"True." His eyes glinted. "And a knighthood for yours truly. It's Sir Charles now, m'dears, so you'll have to treat me with a proper respect."

"Oh, Pa, how wonderful!" Cressida flung her arms around him. "I couldn't be more pleased."

"Yes, well I won't deny it sits rather well with me."

"And, of course, you'll be attending the celebrations at Carlton House."

He chuckled. "Wouldn't miss it for the world, Bea. From all I hear, Prinny has overreached himself this time—sounds like something out of the *Arabian Nights*."

"Really, Charles—what a way to speak of the Prince Regent! Now, then—you will stay with us? Cressida has been so looking forward to seeing you, and Martha can prepare a room in a trice."

"No, no, m'dear. A fine thing it would be an' I came

upsetting all your lives. I'm putting up at the club, for the present, until—the thing is, I am considering acquiring somewhere more permanent, but nothing is finalized as yet."

Sir Charles did not elaborate further, but Cressida knew him too well to be fooled. If he did not have one of his bits of muslin tucked away somewhere, she would be very much surprised, though it would not do to even hint as much to her godmother.

"I hope you have a gown fit for the great occasion, Cressida, m'dear," he said. "Looking forward to showing you off."

Lady Kilbride immediately became flustered. "But Charles, your daughter hasn't yet been presented. What with one thing and another . . ."

"Oh, nothing that can't be overcome with a little ingenuity. Prinny is well pleased with me at the present."

"Then we must visit Madame Fanchon without delay, my child, for it will have to be something special."

"But I have a dozen or more dresses—all eminently suitable."

"Something with a short train, I think," her godmother mused, as though Cressida had not spoken. "Do you not think so, Charles."

"Oh, good Lord, I leave all that sort of thing to you ladies." Sir Charles stood up. "Must be on my way. I'll be in touch." He paused on his way to the door. "Fanchon, did you say?"

"In Conduit Street," Cressida said, suppressing a smile, for the innocent query confirmed her suspicions. "Madame is French—and quite exceptional."

The evening of the reception was everything that Cressida could have imagined—and more. The avenues leading to the supper tents were adorned with grand images depicting themes designed no doubt to appeal to the evening's esteemed guest.

"Which I doubt the great man will even notice," Cressida murmured to Perry.

"One would need to be blind not to notice. You must be pleased to have your father safely home."

She smiled. "Indeed. Not that I have seen much of him since the day he arrived. But it is ever thus with him. I should be with him now, but he was more than usually restless . . . there was someone he had to see . . . I only hope I can find him before we go in to dine. As for his having come home, safe and sound, his restless nature is such that I place no reliance on his remaining long. Except that he was showing some interest in taking a house in town, which I must say surprised me rather, and I did wonder . . ."

Alastair came to join them at that moment, so her thoughts remained unvoiced. He was pleased to compliment her on her gown and for once she could discern no hint of irony in his voice. It was fashioned of a heavy silk in bronze gold with a small train, which showed her fine figure to advantage. And her copper curls had been drawn up into a smooth knot with just a few curls falling loose. He seemed in no hurry to move on, and the three of them whiled away the waiting time in gently ridiculing some of the more outrageous forms of dress.

It was as a small group in front of them moved away that Cressida finally glimpsed her father. As she suspected, he was not alone. The lady clinging to his arm was very beautiful, though not at all in his usual style, for she was heart-stoppingly fair, and fragile of figure, the latter displaying to advantage in a beautiful gown of amber gauze cut almost indecently low at the neck, which bore the unmistakable stamp of Fanchon. So, the mystery was solved.

She turned to share her amusement with her companions and saw that the earl's face was rigidly set, resembling an expressionless mask. She transferred her glance to Perry, whose face gave nothing away.

Yet she was instantly aware that something was gravely amiss.

"So, here you are, m'dear." Sir Charles came across to join them, and was obviously in jovial mood. "There is someone rather special I wish you to meet." He took the lady's hand, his smile resembling that of the cat who had stolen the cream. "Lady Sherbourne—allow me to introduce my very dear daughter, Cressida—the best daughter in the world, without question."

"My father is prone to exaggerate, as you may already have discovered, Lady Sherbourne," Cressida said, as her ladyship offered the tips of her fingers. "I am pleased to meet you."

Large eyes, deep violet in the piquant face, appraised her from beneath dark sweeping lashes, almost as if assessing a rival. "And I have heard much about you," she murmured huskily.

"I'm not sure if you will know Lord Langley—and Mr. Devenham."

"Yes, indeed." Lady Sherbourne smiled and again the fingertips were extended. "Though it must be all of four years since we last met, for I have been in Vienna for three or more years."

"At least four, I would say." Alastair's voice was silky smooth as their hands touched briefly, and his profile might have been chiselled out of ice, so coldly still it was. Cressida looked from one to the other.

"This is a splendid occasion, is it not?" Perry murmured in his gentle way. "It quite restores one's faith in the heights of fancy and pomposity to which princes may aspire, if turned loose upon the world."

As if to prove Perry's point, Count von Schroder came pushing his way through the crowds to her side, a chestful of medals pinned to his dress uniform.

"Miss Merriton, what a pleasure it is to see you here. I had hoped."

She forced herself to greet him politely. "With so

many people present, it is a wonder anyone can find anyone."

There was a stirring in the crowd, the sound of an unmistakable jovial voice, a whooping laugh, and the crowds parted as a familiar figure came into view.

"The great man himself, the savior of us all," the count murmured, his tone derisive. "One would not think it possible, just by looking at him."

"Perhaps not." She forced herself to be polite. "But that surely applies to most truly great men."

The duke caught sight of her and came forward to shake her hand vigorously as she congratulated him.

"Miss Cressida . . . yes, indeed, this is indeed a great day . . . You'll be pleased to see your father home and in good heart, no doubt . . . and both of us gone up in the world . . ." He laughed again and moved on to have a brief word with her father, then he was gone.

"You are honored," Perry said with his quiet smile.

"Why, so I think."

"Now that our long-awaited special guest has arrived, it seems we are to move forward," Sir Charles observed jovially, unaware of the moods and tensions he had set in train. "And I am in the fortunate position of having a beautiful woman on each arm."

Cressida paused to look back with renewed concern at Alastair, only to find him laughing at some remark of Perry's as though he hadn't a care in the world, so that she wondered if she had imagined his coldness.

It had been an altogether extraordinary evening she decided much later, as she lay in bed, wide-awake, reliving the spectacle as she had joined the many eminent people processing through the house to be confronted at last by an immense and quite breathtaking edifice, designed and built to the Regent's wishes by John Nash, where a huge banquet had been prepared. It had also been an exhilarating, unsettling evening, full of unanswered questions. But as she finally drifted into sleep, her last coherent memory was of Alastair's curiously blank face as Pa had introduced his latest *chère amie*.

Chapter Nine

Lady Kilbride was not by nature an early riser, but on the morning following the Carlton House reception she was awake and eager to hear all about it from Cressida. And she was not disappointed. She sat up in bed in her nightcap and shawl, dipping fingers of toasted bread into her hot chocolate, and chuckling as Cressida gave her a graphic and highly entertaining account of the previous evening with all its absurdities.

"I would not have missed it for the world, dear ma'am, for it was by far and away beyond anything I could have conjured up out of my imagination. I wish you could have seen the banqueting hall, with its ceiling fashioned like a huge parasol, and painted to resemble the soft muslin draping the walls. And the avenues leading to it lined with transparencies depicting valiant themes. Pa told me that the Prince Regent had it designed and built especially for the occasion."

"It certainly sounds magnificent. And I am sure I have heard that His Royal Highness has a passionate interest in design and all things decorative."

"Then he should be well pleased. The duke of Wellington, as he now is, was in high good humour and was kind enough to spare a word for me. In fact, with Pa known to absolutely everyone who is anyone, I was in danger of being spoiled. Even the Regent, who is immensely fat, but quite charming, remembered me. And Lady Jersey has promised to send me vouchers for Almack's, which Perry says I must consider almost as great an honour—though I suspect he was teasing."

"Never say so, my dear. The patronesses of Almack's have a great deal of influence on society, and one offends them at one's peril. Vouchers are not given to everyone, I assure you." Lady Beatrice looked into the upturned face, glowing with lingering enjoyment, and wondered how she would go on when Cressida left her, as she must do someday. She sighed. "I vow you will have all the young men queuing up to dance with you."

Cressida laughed. "I don't know about that. But I am resolved not to let it go to my head, for I am of the opinion that it is all a kind of game. Oh, and another thing I must tell you—I was right about Papa—he has found himself a new inamorata—a veritable beauty, as alluring as any creature out of a romantic legend."

"My dear!" Lady Beatrice was shocked by such outspokenness. Young ladies in her day would scarce have known about such matters, let alone voice their opinions in the presence of their elders. But then, she supposed that as Cressida had led a less than conventional life, one was obliged to make allowances. In the end curiosity won the day. "Though to be sure, I cannot say it comes as any surprise, for he had ever an eye for a pretty woman, which is not to say that his love for your dear mama was not something quite exceptional."

"Indeed I know that, ma'am. And I am certain that while she lived, he never strayed—or hardly ever," she amended, striving for honesty, "and if he did, he was always discreet for he would not have hurt her for the world . . ."

Unlike me, Lady Beatrice thought. But the memory was fleeting now, and quite without pain, for it was all such a long time ago when he had been young and heedless of love's power to wound.

"It frequently astonishes me that he somehow manages to remain on cordial terms with most of his inamoratas." Cressida selected a particularly luscious-looking fig from the comfit dish. "Though this latest is not quite in his usual style, for in general his preference is for voluptuous dark-eyed beauties, and one could not by any stretch of the imagination describe Lady Sherbourne in such terms, for she is quite wonderfully fair, and I suspect her appeal lies in her apparent fragility . . ." Cressida stopped, aware that her godmother had turned quite pale, one hand clasped to her breast in her agitation. "Dear ma'am, is something wrong? Have I shocked you? Or are you unwell?"

"Did you say Lady Sherbourne? It cannot be . . . oh, do tell me you mistook the name."

"No. There can be no mistake," Cressida said, completely mystified by her godmother's reactions. "Pa introduced me to her. In any case, she seemed to be known to a number of people—in fact, I had the distinct impression that her presence had caused something of a stir."

"Oh, my poor boy!"

"Pa? He is hardly a boy—or poor, for that matter."

"No, no! I speak of Alastair!"

Her curiosity by now thoroughly aroused, Cressida found herself remembering how his face had that look of cold reserve. "Now that you mention it, I suppose he did seem to be somewhat taken aback—but only for a moment, so briefly, in fact, that I supposed I had imagined it. But how is Alastair concerned?" Lady Kilbride was slow to answer, a handkerchief pressed against her mouth. "Pray do not feel obliged to say anything if it distresses you."

"That woman! She went away—to Vienna, so I heard." It was as if her godmother was talking to herself, and with a bitterness that seemed quite foreign to her. "Oh, why could she not have stayed away!"

Cressida's curiosity was growing by the minute, but

she managed to restrain it, saying calmly, "You know her, then? And obviously dislike her. Perhaps I should not have told you, but truly, there was no great drama. As for Alastair—I doubt his reaction was due to anything other than surprise."

"Shock, more like," her godmother declared with unaccustomed venom. "That woman broke his heart—ridiculed him for all to see—changed him overnight from a charming, devil-may-care young man to a cynical care-for-nothing. So much so that I doubt he will ever wholly trust a woman again."

Lady Kilbride's explanation would certainly account for Alastair's seeming coolness of manner, though there had been moments, as in the long gallery at Langley House, when, just for a few moments, he had lowered his guard, and she had been vouchsafed a glimpse of a very different man. Prudence dictated that she ought not to pursue so delicate a subject, but by now curiosity had won the day.

"How dreadful! Would it distress you to tell me what happened? For Pa would seem to have put me in a very difficult position." And not just me, she thought, for only suppose Pa wished Lady Sherbourne to be invited to the ball.

For a moment it seemed that her godmother might find the telling too painful. But then, with a sigh, she began. "It must be all of five years ago that Lady Alice Waring, as she then was, came to town to stay with an aunt, for her parents had both died some years previously in a tragic accident—or so we were led to believe. She was just turned eighteen and quite lovely, though I cannot say I ever took to her, for in spite of her youth and undoubted beauty there was something acquisitive about her. But Alastair was head over ears in love with her from the first moment he saw her, and blind to any hint of a fault. And Alice gave every appearance of returning his love. They were the talk of London that spring, and within weeks they were betrothed. I begged Alastair not to rush into marriage, but in those days he was a very different person—impetuous and deaf to all advice. The wedding plans were well in hand when Lord Sherbourne came on the scene. He was old enough to be Alice's grandfather, but he was immensely rich and in the market for a pretty young wife, and I suppose the temptation proved too much for her. In fact, I doubt if she gave Alastair more than a passing thought, for within a month or so she and Sherbourne were married. And within a twelvemonth he was dead, and she an exceedingly wealthy woman. I believe she went abroad to avoid having to wait out her period of mourning." Lady Beatrice sighed. "And now she is back—and my poor boy will have to endure the ignominy having his past resurrected."

Oh, what a coil! Cressida thought, returning at last to her room, only to pace restlessly. No wonder Alastair had grown a protective shell. For, to have been so cruelly rejected must surely account for that wariness in him which she had sensed from the first. But had she known the whole tragic saga, she would not have confided so readily in her godmother. Why, oh why, could her parent's roving eye not have lighted on some harmless light-o'-love?

"You'll wear that strip of carpet out, the way you're pacin' up and down," Jane Batty complained. "I thought you'd still be abed, the time you came home last night—or rather, this morning."

"I thought you knew me better than that. I never lie abed. It's no good—I can't settle. You'd better bring me my riding habit, then send word for Manuel to saddle Vitoria and bring him round."

It was still early enough to have Rotten Row almost to herself, and with the sun on her back, she was able to work off some of her frustrations with a brief invigorating gallop, before reverting to a more decorous pace, with Manuel keeping a discreet distance behind.

But her solitude was destined not to last, for presently she heard a horseman coming up fast behind her, and she was hailed by an all too familiar voice.

"Miss Merriton—I knew at once that it must be you." Count von Schroder drew alongside, his fleshy face sweating slightly from his exertions. "Most young ladies would still be abed after such an evening, but I flatter myself that I know enough of your character to be certain that you would scorn any such hint of frailty. Not that I approve of young ladies being accorded so much licence."

There was a gratuitous smugness about his pronouncement that, as always, made her long to prick the bubble of his conceit. Except that he was so thick-skinned as to render any such feat well nigh impossible. It was much to her relief, therefore, that she saw a horseman in the distance, riding fast.

"Do forgive me, Count," she said, gathering up her reins. "Your views on women are illuminating, if archaic. But I cannot stay to argue with you, for if I am not mistaken, Lord Langley is about to enter the park, and I very much wish to speak with him."

"I would advise against it, for I doubt you will find him good company." There was a note of barbed ridicule in the count's voice. "Least of all where you are concerned, for if you will forgive my being . . . a trifle indelicate, I believe your esteemed parent has placed his lordship in a most embarrassing position—and one which, last evening, was everywhere being discussed."

There was a smugness about the comment that made her long to crack her whip across his face. Instead, she said coolly, "If you say so. I was not aware of it. But then, I make it a practice never to listen to gossip, especially if it is of a scurrilous nature." She felt a small glow of satisfaction as she watched his face become suffused with colour. "And now, if you will forgive me . . ." She signalled to Manuel to follow and rode away.

Anger lent speed to her flight, and once in the park she quickly caught up with Alastair whose pace was now reduced to a gentle canter. As she drew closer, he looked back to see who was following, and after a moment, slowed to allow her to come up to him.

"Thank goodness I saw you," she said. "I had been accosted by Count von Schroder, and was desperate to find some means of escape."

"Poor count." His voice lacked expression, giving little indication of his mood.

"Poor nothing! He is the most pompous, hubristic and unlikeable man it has ever been my misfortune to meet. His views on women and their place in life are positively archaic."

"And you doubtless told him so?"

"Of course."

He frowned. "I doubt that was wise, but you seem to have a penchant for speaking first and thinking later."

"Not true," she swiftly countered. "But I do believe in speaking my mind when challenged."

His frown deepened. "Which could be downright dangerous with a man like Count von Schroder. However, I am coming to realise that you take a delight in courting danger, so it is pointless for us to argue."

"Quite," she said. The curtness of his reproof had stung, but she refused to be intimidated.

They rode in silence for a few moments, and whilst she was still wondering how best to say what she wished to say, he spoke again, in a slightly more conciliating tone. "I am surprised to see you about so early after Prinny's grand *pièce de resistance,* though I am fast coming to learn that nothing about you should surprise me."

"Pooh! I do not count this as early. As a general rule I need very little sleep. And after such a stimulating evening, I found myself more wide awake than usual. Besides, it is such a lovely morning."

He did not immediately answer her.

"However, if you would rather be on your own, pray do not hesitate to say so," she said, feeling a trifle piqued. "You must know by now that my skin is very thick, so I shall not be in the least offended."

His abrupt laugh lacked humour. "What an extraordinary girl you are."

"Do you think so? I am not sure whether that may be considered a compliment or not, but I shall take it as one." They rode on in a slightly tense silence for a while, until finally she broke it to say, almost tentatively for her, "Do you think we might walk for a little? Manuel will hold the horses."

He frowned and she thought he would refuse. Then, with a shrug, he acquiesced. They walked in silence whilst she wondered how to broach so delicate a subject. Finally she decided to come straight out with it.

"The thing is, there is something I wish to say."

"I supposed there might be. But you had much better not," he said crisply.

"You may be right." She drew a deep breath. "However, even at the risk of incurring your wrath, I cannot remain silent." She paused, expecting him to argue. When he did not, she continued. "The thing is, I could hardly fail to be aware of the fact that my father, however inadvertently, caused you some considerable embarrassment last night. I am sure he would not have done so, had he known."

"You have been talking to Aunt Beatrice."

His voice had a clipped note that should have warned her to have a care. Instead, it put her on the defensive. "I do not indulge in tittle-tattle," she said crisply. "In fact, had I known I would not have—but that is neither here nor there. I was simply regaling your aunt with the events of the evening in general, and thought to amuse her by telling her about Pa's latest inamorata." She could deduce little from his taut profile, but when he said nothing, she continued with some spirit, "Well, how was I to know? But as it turned out, poor Lady Bea was quite overcome and because of her great fondness for you, the whole story poured out."

"No doubt much embellished by my aunt's love of melodrama." There was a harshness in his voice.

"Perhaps—a little. She is very fond of you," Cressida protested.

"Which can in itself be something of a trial, for she has convinced herself that my heart was irrevocably broken when Alice ran off with Sherbourne. And nothing will persuade her otherwise."

"But then I suspect that Lady Bea is a romantic at heart. Also she knows only too well how it feels to be cast aside for someone else . . ."

"That will do!" He seized her by the shoulders and turned her to face him. His eyes were frightening pinpoints of light, and there was a rawness in his voice that should have warned her not to proceed. But having gone so far, she screwed up her courage to finish. "Whereas for you it was quite different," she concluded, head up and looking him full in the eyes, which was a mistake for their expression was enough to frighten the bravest of creatures.

"Really? In what way?" His voice had taken on a silky quality.

"It doesn't matter."

His fingers tightened their grip. "In what way?" he repeated.

Cressida's heart was beating very fast, but she was also growing angry. She lifted her head and looked him full in his cold hard eyes. "Because, in my experience," she said frankly, "it is easy for a young man to assuage his heartbreak, or hurt pride, in the time-honoured way. Young ladies are not afforded any such luxury. They are left to weep alone—as your aunt was."

He should have been—indeed was, he told himelf—

furious. For a long moment he continued to hold her, subjecting her to an intense and lingering scrutiny, which came to rest on the stubborn set of her sweetly curving mouth. And quite spontaneously experienced an almost overwhelming desire to crush it into submission. For a long moment they stood, unmoving, their glances locked. Then sanity returned. He released his grip and stepped back—so suddenly that she almost fell.

"You really are quite the most outrageous, opinionated, meddlesome young woman it has ever been my misfortune to meet . . ."

There were tears half blinding her eyes, blocking her throat, but she forced them back to look him full in the face. "Perhaps I am. But I am seldom wrong." She turned away to where Manuel waited with the horses, his curiosity hardly concealed. "Help me up, Manuel," she said, "I am ready to go home."

He hesitated, unsure how to accomplish her wishes without also relinquishing hold of his lordship's horse. And whilst he hesitated, Alastair was beside her, his expression still rigid as he tossed her into the saddle. She looked down at him, her eyes over-bright. "As for Pa, your aunt worries needlessly, for I doubt the Lady Alice will succeed in entrapping him for long. His capacity for constancy is woefully inadequate— much more so even than hers."

This drew from him an abrupt laugh. "What a very unfilial daughter you are. Do you know him so well?"

"Oh, yes."

He watched her ride away, and then, with a smothered curse, mounted his own horse and followed her.

Cressida head him coming, but made no attempt to quicken her pace as he came abreast of her. They rode in silence for a moment or two, then he said forcefully, "Damn it, this is ridiculous. Let us, for pity's sake, call 'quits.' "

"With pleasure, my lord," she agreed. "I have no desire to quarrel."

"Then so be it." For a while neither spoke. Then he said with a shade more warmth in his voice, "You may care to know that the arrangements for the ball are now complete. All five hundred guests have accepted, and we shall sit down twenty to dinner."

"Goodness!" she exclaimed.

"Perhaps you could spare an hour or so from your increasingly busy life to go through the final details with me sometime."

She decided to ignore the hint of irony in his voice. "Yes, of course. Whenever you wish."

Chapter Ten

Cressida's suggestion that she might take an active interest in overseeing the final preparations for the dinner filled Alastair with horror.

"Out of the question," he said. "You don't know my *chef de cuisine*, Henri Baptiste. He would never allow a woman to invade his territory."

"Then I must do my best to persuade him that I pose no threat. Also that I do have some considerable experience, for Pa always left such matters to me."

"I doubt that will carry much weight with Henri Baptiste."

"But I may try?"

He threw her a look that was half-quizzical, half-impatient. "Are you always so stubborn?"

"Determined," she said. "And only when I am like to be thwarted. If I could just convince your *chef de cuisine* that I am quite harmless, I'm sure we would get along very well."

"I can see there is no reasoning with you. But if he gives notice, I shall hold you personally responsible."

At first it seemed that Alastair would be proved right. Henri Baptiste, though small and stocky of figure, managed to be fearsomely imposing. His glassy-eyed stare as the earl obliged him to cooperate with Cressida did not bode well.

"*Non!* It is impossible."

"Then you will make it possible, Henri Baptiste," the earl replied coldly.

There was a small silence, a stiffening of shoulders—a look toward the ceiling. Then: "I believe Lady Colchester is in need of a *chef de cuisine*. I 'ave been approached."

"I'm sure you have. The choice is yours, of course, though I doubt you would care to work for her. I am told she is incredibly hard to please and never keeps anyone more than a month or two. However . . ." The silence stretched until Cressida could stand it no longer.

"This is quite ridiculous. Henri Baptiste, I have no wish to do other than be allowed to observe what I am assured is a skill beyond price. It sometimes falls to me to arrange dinner parties for my father, and I have heard your praises so highly sung that I am eager to learn from a master."

For a moment her words hung in the air. Then, with a Gallic shrug, he capitulated.

"I shall leave you to it, then," murmured Alastair, and for Cressida's ears only, "I congratulate you. Talk about tipping the butter boat." She had the grace to blush. "And don't forget your *frisseur* is due at six o'clock."

Left alone with Henry Baptiste, she did her best to smooth ruffled feathers. "Although I am a mere amateur, I do understand how you must feel, for there is nothing more guaranteed to undermine one's creativity than to be forever having someone peering over one's shoulder. But his lordship was so high in his praise for you that I longed to watch a master at work. And this is, after all, my special night."

Henri Baptiste, his ruffled feathers smoothed, his ego restored, was disposed to be generous. This was clearly no ordinary mademoiselle. She had a definite presence. And if one were to credit the gossip of the lower orders, which he naturally did not, it was even conceivable that she might one day be mistress of this house. So it would be wise to tread carefully.

"Eh bien," he said with just the right degree of condescension, "for this once we will make the exception."

The hour that followed was truly engrossing as Cressida watched the total transformation of the dining room, the table sparkling with silver and finest cut glass. And at its center a huge silver epergne fragrant with flowers, which she had been permitted to help arrange under Henri Baptiste's watchful eye. The chef had mellowed as the afternoon wore on, as his opinion of her was confirmed. Also, her enthusiasm was infectious—and her appreciation of his *pièce de resistance*— a huge castle of snowy white meringue surrounded by a moat of crème chantilly where tiny doves bobbed— was quite genuine. All this and more convinced him that his master could do much worse, should the gossips prove to be right.

But all too soon she was obliged to leave. "Thank you, Henri Baptiste," she said warmly, "for your generosity. I have learned so much from you."

"It was a pleasure, mademoiselle," he replied, and was surprised to find that he meant it.

On her way to the room put at her disposal for the evening, she looked into the ballroom and found it transformed. What had seemed disappointing by day, had now become a brilliant illusion of light and space. An army of servants had been busy lighting the Venetian chandeliers, and all that had seemed disappointing by day, was now magically altered, for as each sprang into life, they were transformed, their lusters moving with the draught from the open door, and their beauty was reflected and intensified in the mirrored panels that lined the walls.

"Do you approve?" Alastair's voice startled her.

"Oh, yes," she said softly.

"The chandeliers were commisioned by my father and brought from Venice for his wedding. They are, I believe, unique."

"I'm sure they are. I have never seen anything half so fine." She hesitated, then said impulsively, "I'm not sure whether I have ever thanked you adequately for all of this—" She waved an arm. "I have sometimes felt that Lady Bea pressured you into helping her . . ."

"Then you worry needlessly," he said abruptly. "I never do anything I don't wish to do—even to please Aunt Bea. As for this evening, I take it you and Henri Baptiste have managed to survive without coming to cuffs?"

"Indeed, yes. In fact, by the time I left him, we had reached a tolerable state of understanding. And now, forgive me, I must go. The poor *frisseur* will be tearing his hair. Oh, dear, I'm sorry, that was a terrible pun."

As the door closed behind her, she was sure she heard him laugh.

From that moment on, she scarce had time to think. But by the time Lady Beatrice arrived and came panting up the beautiful staircase, she was almost ready.

"My dear, you look quite lovely," her ladyship exclaimed. "You will break all hearts. Madame Fanchon has truly excelled herself!"

Cressida was by now used to her godmother's flights of fancy, but for once she had to admit that Lady Bea had not exaggerated. She subjected her reflection in the long mirror to a critical eye, twisting this way and that until Jane Batty, who was still struggling to fasten the long row of tiny pearl buttons down the back of the gown exclaimed sharply, "Be still, Miss Cressida, for pity's sake—or I'll never be done."

Lady Beatrice looked shocked at the maid's familiarity, but Cressida only laughed and seemed to see nothing strange in it.

The gown was indeed a triumphant blend of simplicity and sophistication. The brief ruched bodice with its tiny puffed sleeves, was fashioned of ivory gauze and scattered with tiny gold acorns, and from it a gown of heavy gold silk skimmed the contours of her figure to sway in whispering folds about her feet.

"And as for your hair . . . if you had told me you were to have it cut so short, I would have been appalled, but really, it is quite charming."

'I had not intended to, but Monsieur Claude was very persuasive. Apparently, it is the very latest fashion." And indeed, it was highly becoming, for although she had almost panicked to see so much of her precious hair fall to the floor, the remainder now clustered quite charmingly around a delicate circlet of gold filigree—a present from Pa.

"Exquisite. But then, Charles ever had impeccable taste," Lady Kilbride said—and found herself blushing like a young girl as she watched him approach, relieved to see that he had left Lady Sherbourne deep in conversation with that pompous Austrian count. Charles was still a very fine figure of a man, she thought with blatant partiality, despite the slight thickening of his fine figure, which his height rendered negligible. And as always he was in jovial mood.

"Well, Cressida, m'dear," he said, taking her hands in his and standing back to admire her. "You outshine them all, damned if you don't. Y'r mother would have been so proud to see this day—" He half turned. "Ain't that so, Bea?"

Her ladyship drew a quick breath and swallowed hard. "Yes, indeed. There are times when I see much of Arabella in dear Cressida. She is a constant joy to have about the place."

Perry was equally appreciative in his quiet way. "Never seen you look finer, m'dear—truly the belle of the ball. I hope you mean to honor me with a dance?"

"But of course." Cressida's eyes were alight with laughter. "My card is filling up fast. Alastair has already bespoken the supper waltz, but I still have a boulanger remaining and the second quadrille."

"Such is your popularity," he replied, giving her a

gentle smile. "How you are gone up in the world. Shall we say the quadrille?"

The dinner had been a spectacular success, which even the presence of Lady Sherbourne at her father's side could not diminish. In fact, to all outward appearances Alastair seemed to have accepted her ladyship's presence with equanimity. As the guests for the ball assembled, Harry Pelham had bespoken the boulanger—"If you will n-not mind a fellow being a little clumsy," he said diffidently, and was instantly reassured. So her card was full, and it was clear that the dinner had set a precedent for the whole evening. Even Lady Kilbride was unusually relaxed as she sat with Lady Jersey and dear Lady Sefton.

In the ballroom the orchestra was already tuning up and Sir Charles prepared to lead Cressida out in the opening cotillion. "Father's privilege," he said jovially, and turning to Alastair, "And you, my boy, may have the pleasure of partnering my Alice. She's an accomplished little dancer."

In the infinitessimal pause that followed, Cressida hardly dared to look at Alastair. Then, "It will be my pleasure, sir," he said with infinite politeness, and extended a hand. "Lady Sherbourne."

She put her hand in his and smiled provocatively up at him. "My lord."

There was nothing to be done, and indeed, it seemed that she had worried unnecessarily, for in the odd glimpses she caught of them they seemed to be dealing in reasonable accord.

Later, when Alastair came to claim her for the supper dance, she did attempt to venture a kind of apology on behalf of her father, who was in ignorance of the situation, but he cut her short.

"You worry unnecessarily, my dear Cressida. There really is no need."

"I'm glad," she said, but did not believe him for one moment. There was a tautness in him, an unnatural brilliance in his eyes which suggested he many have drunk rather more than usual.

The music was insidiously romantic and the chandeliers appeared to spin above as Alastair whirled her around, ever faster, dipping and swaying. She was exquisitely aware of his closeness, of the intimate warmth of his hand through the silk of her gown. Was it of her he thought, or Alice?

The music swept to a triumphant close—and with it returned a measure of sanity. "You dance well," he said, releasing her rather too abruptly.

"I had an accomplished partner," she said lightly, and hoped he would not detect the fast beating of her heart.

Lady Kilbride, watching them from her place on the little dais with Lady Sefton, felt her heart quicken a little. If only . . . surely there was more than the usual partiality between these two young people who meant so much to her? That would fulfil all her dreams.

But the surprises were not yet over, for when, just before supper, the duke of Wellington arrived, bringing with him the duke of York, and stayed a full half hour, Lady Kilbride's cup was full to overflowing.

"A stroke of genius, Alastair," she exclaimed. "However did you manage it?"

"Nothing to do with me, Aunt Bea. I fear you credit me with too much influence," he said. "It is Sir Charles you should be thanking."

"Of course. I should have guessed. It seems there is no one he does not know." Her ladyship blushed and looked flustered. "However, it has certainly set the seal on the whole evening."

Much later, after supper, Cressida was sitting beside Lady Sefton as she waited for the dancing to begin again. Her ladyship was extolling the excellence of the music provided by the Scots Greys throughout supper, and as her attention began to wander, she became aware of Count von Schroder striding purposefully toward them.

"I believe you about to acquire yet another admirer, my dear," her ladyship murmured, her eyes twinkling. "And a rather determined one, by the look of him. Such an impressive uniform. Very Teutonic. You have been very kind, but you mustn't let me keep you. This is your special evening, after all."

Count von Schroder stopped before them, clicked his heels, and bowed with military precision as he greeted both ladies before turning back to Cressida.

"Miss Merriton—at last. My apologies. I have been detained by a family matter."

"No apology is necessary, Count. Shall we walk a little? I hope your problem was resolved satisfactorily?"

"A small matter of discipline—but one which would not wait." There was something in the way he said it that sent a slight shiver down her back. But his mind was already on more important matters. "I trust I am not too late to claim a dance?"

"Oh, dear," she said, trying to sound suitably disappointed. "I'm afraid you are. My card was filled so quickly, you see."

His brow was like thunder. "Surely not?"

"Indeed, I am sorry. But you need not go short of a partner." In the background the orchestra could be heard tuning up. "If you hurry, I'm sure you will find several ladies present who would consider it a privilege to dance the waltz with you."

"But I do not wish . . ." He struggled to contain his ire.

"And here, I believe, is Harry Pelham come to claim his boulanger."

The count was thunderstruck. "You would prefer that pathetic creature to me?"

Cressida drew a deep breath, not knowing how she kept her temper. "Harry is my friend. And far from being pathetic, he is also one of the bravest men I know." She stopped and turned to him. "I do hope you will find a suitable partner, Count."

He bowed punctiliously, and strode away, stiff-backed. "I say, Cressida . . . I d-didn't butt in, did I? Von Schroder I l-looked mad as fire."

"On the contrary." She linked her arm through Harry's. "I have often suspected that the good count always looks as mad as fire when he doesn't get his own way. A dangerous man to cross, in fact. You came in the nick of time."

Chapter Eleven

"My dear, you are made! Depend upon it, there will scarce be anyone of note who will not be clamoring to invite Miss Merriton to their balls and routs—and goodness knows where it all may lead."

Cressida had returned from her customary early-morning ride, expecting to find her godmother in bed in a state of exhaustion. Instead, the good lady was sitting up and making an excellent breakfast.

"If, before the morning is out, the mantelshelf is not littered with invitations, I shall be very surprised. I could not have wished for better."

"Then for your sake I hope you may be right," Cressida said, her mind only half on her godmother's chatter—the other half still mulling over a disturbing incident which had arisen out of her ride in Green Park. When she first entered, the park had seemed deserted except for a small herd of cows peacefully grazing in the far distance. But presently she observed two figures close together beneath a canopy of trees. An early-morning lovers' tryst, perhaps, she thought, and was about to cut away across the grass when something familiar about the pair made her pause and rein in.

They were far too engrossed to have noticed her. Alastair she could not mistake, but his companion was female, much slighter, and almost totally enveloped in a hooded cloak. Cressida's immediate thought was that it might be Lady Sherbourne. If so, her presence could well cause embarrassment to both parties, as well as herself, especially as they seemed to be arguing. At one point Alastair even took hold of the woman's shoulders as if to shake her, and she seemed to wince as she struggled to free herself. It was at that moment that the hood fell back a little, and the lady was revealed; it was not Lady Sherbourne, but the pretty Miss Isabella Devine—now a very troubled and not quite so pretty Miss Devine, for even at a distance Cressida could see that one side of her face was badly bruised. Aware that their argument was none of her business and that she ought to retrace her path quietly, she yet remained, intrigued by the curious tableau. And as she watched, Isabella pulled away, shook her head violently, cried, "No, no, I can't!" and wrapping her cloak around her, turned and ran.

It seemed certain that Alastair must follow her, but instead he simply watched her go, and in a fit of what Cressida took to be temper, slammed his riding crop against a nearby tree. It was so out of character that she became more than ever intrigued. As he turned to untie his horse she walked Vitoria forward.

"Good morning, Alastair. We are both out early, it seems."

He looked up at her, his face still thunderous. "The devil! Do you never sleep?"

"You were more polite last night."

"Last night." He struggled to master his feelings. "Yes, of course. Forgive my appalling manners. The ball went very well, I think. I hope your father was pleased."

"Yes, indeed. He was delighted."

"I had not expected to see you about so soon."

"Nor I, you. But then, we are both by nature early risers, are we not?" Cressida dismounted and Vitoria, his energies for the moment satisfied, shook his head and stood still. She hesitated, then said in a more conciliatory tone, "Forgive me—I do not mean to pry,

but was that not Miss Devine I saw hurrying away?
She seemed much troubled—an accident, perhaps. I
could have sworn her face was bruised."

He did not answer at once.

"Pa always says I am by far too inquisitive and overeager to rescue lame ducks," she went on, deciding to
brave his possible annoyance at her interference, "so
you are quite at liberty to tell me to mind my own
business. But although she is exceedingly pretty and
vivacious, Miss Devine is rather naive, is she not? And
her current involvement with von Schroder is hardly
a secret. I confess that the very thought of it disturbs
me. I believe I told you that the count was in Lisbon
while I was there. He cut a fine figure in society, and
was much admired by the ladies, although I always
found him too full of hubris for my liking. However,
many of my friends confessed that, given the chance,
they would be only too eager to succumb to his particular brand of charm, with its tantalizing hint of danger.
But I had heard rather too many unsavory rumours
concerning his treatment of women and something he
let slip in conversation last night alarmed me. It also
made me wonder—in short, if you have any influence
with Miss Devine, I beg you will use it before she has
cause to regret the connection."

For a moment she thought she had offended him
further, then he muttered, "Oh, hell and the devil!"
and immediately apologized for his language.

"Pray, don't even consider it. Pa swears all the time.
Do I take it my warning comes too late?"

"I fear so, though Isabella stopped short of admitting it. It was quite by chance that I came upon her
just now, taking the air when she thought the park
would be deserted. The poor girl is obviously terrified
of von Schroder, but will not heed me. I don't know
what threats he has used against her . . ."

"From certain rumors I once heard, he doesn't need
to threaten. He is like a snake—if his current mistress

displeases him, he will thrash her, then salve her bruises, make passionate love to her, and she will be enslaved once more."

"Good God! The man must be a monster!"

"Quite. But some women, so I'm told, are natural victims. Could this be true of Miss Devine, do you suppose?"

He frowned, as if considering the question. "I know little of her background, except that she was supposedly orphaned as a child and lived with an aunt—a very strange woman, by all accounts, who left her very much to her own devices—and whose only advice to her once she reached a suitable age and in the absence of any dowry, was to find herself a rich provider. And, being capricious as well as pretty, she has until now managed to charm her way into the affections of several willing gentlemen who have treated her well."

And were you one of them? Cressida wondered.

"Not I, as it happens," he said, reading her mind. "I might have been tempted, had her attempts to lure me been less obvious."

"For shame."

"Perhaps it would have been better for her if I had. She would not then have fallen into von Schroder's clutches."

"Nonsense. That is a spurious argument," Cressida retorted. "Her character was most likely formed from birth. It is often so, I believe. However, that is neither here nor there. The most urgent problem we have now is to find some way of removing her from that man's clutches."

He fixed her with an awesome frown. "When you say 'we,' I hope you don't seek to involve me in your schemes."

"Well, I do think you might at least give the situation some thought, for it is quite obvious that matters cannot be left as they are. Next time, that monster may not stop at bruises, and who knows—between us, we may be able to find a solution."

With that much decided, and Vitoria becoming skittish, she said, "And now, if you would give me a hand up, I think we had better ride on."

"Do you make a habit of ordering other people's lives?" he asked as they made their way back to Mount Street.

"Only when it is patently obvious that they are unable to work things out for themselves."

"Of course." The irony in his voice was unmistakable. "Why did I not think of that?"

"And I have never hurt anyone that I know of. In general, people are only too pleased to have their problems solved."

"If you say so."

They parted on reasonably amicable terms, though without any definite plans for the resolution of Isabella Devine's seemingly impossible situation. Lady Kilbride was in the salon when Cressida returned, leafing through a small pile of calling cards.

"What did I tell you, my dear—there must be all of a dozen or more invitations here and the day not half-over. Everything from rout parties to grand balls! It is a triumph! We must drive to the park this afternoon, for everyone will be talking about the ball and wishing to meet you."

"Oh, surely not!" Cressida protested. But later that day in the park it was apparent that her godmother's predictions were nothing less than accurate. It was a perfect summer day, thus coaxing everyone who was anyone to venture forth, and for those fortunate enough to have attended the ball, there was only one topic of conversation. Lady Kilbride positively glowed with pride as her carriage was constantly stopped so that congratulations might be showered upon her— and her godchild. And as for Cressida herself, she was quite genuinely surprised to find herself the object of so much attention.

"Your name is on everyone's lips," Perry said. "Depend upon it, you have made a *succes fou*."

"It is very gratifying, of course," she said, refusing to take him seriously. "And if Lady Bea is happy, then I am happy. Though I doubt it will be anything more than a nine day wonder."

"Such phlegm, egad!" He put up his glass. "You take it all very calmly, I must say."

She laughed. "Well, how would you have me take it? I am under no illusion concerning my newfound popularity. Everything, after all, is in my favor. I am well connected and have Lady Bea for my sponsor—my father is an important man and a crony of the duke of Wellington—and Lord Langley puts himself out to host a ball for me. With such a pedigree, I must surely be in demand."

Perry chuckled. "I can see there is little danger of any undue flattery going to your head."

"Gracious, no. If there were the least sign of any such pretensions, Pa would nip them firmly in the bud."

"And Alastair?"

"Oh, you are more likely than I to divine Alastair's thoughts on the matter. But when we met earlier this morning he seemed well satisfied."

As she spoke her eyes lifted to see him standing no more than a few yards away, his head inclined toward a vision in palest lavender, her head lifted beneath a high poke bonnet to display a cluster of pale gold curls. To Cressida it seemed that the two of them were totally absorbed in one another. She told herself that the dismay she felt was on her father's behalf, though she knew full well that Pa was more than able to order his own affairs.

"Things ain't always what they seem, y'know,"

Perry murmured beside her, intrigued by her reference to an early-morning meeting.

"Quite so," she said briskly. "In any case, he would not thank me for interfering."

Chapter Twelve

Harry Pelham was finding it difficult to come to grips with the possible termination of his army career, for it was virtually the only life he had known. He had grown up in India, where his father had been adjutant to the then Colonel Wellesley. His mother had died of a fever when he was two, and he had been brought up by an ayah who, though kind, had provided little stimulation for a growing boy. In consequence he had become self-sufficient at an early age, impatient only for the day when he would be old enough to enlist as the lowliest of drummer boys, refusing any favors that might have been granted to him as his father's son. He was, if anything, treated more harshly than the other boys—perhaps because of who he was, and also because he was by nature rather serious for his years, and had an unfortunate stammer that was much ridiculed. But he had accepted the jibes philosophically as part of his training for a future in which discipline might make the difference between life and death, and rose steadily through the ranks.

By the time he attained the rank of major, he had seen more action than most of his contemporaries and had during the Peninsular campaign earned himself something of a reputation as a scout, frequently infiltrating enemy territory single-handed, a feat that suited his reserved disposition and had earned him several commendations for bravery until his luck finally ran out when a stray cannon shot took off his arm.

By then the war was all but over and with it came a sense of anticlimax for the thought of becoming some kind of tame equerry, which was probably the only position he could hope for, filled him with despair and a kind of inner rage, fuelled by the pity that lurked so often behind the false jollity of embarrassed acquaintances who weren't sure how to treat him. Only a few—a very few like Cressida Merriton—could even begin to understand how he felt.

It was in this bleak mood that he walked along by the Serpentine early one morning. The rising sun was tinting the water, reminding him of the River Douro, blood-red with barrels of wine blown up in battle.

His attention was presently caught by a slight figure wrapped in an all-enveloping cloak a little way ahead of him, who had stopped and was staring down intently. There was something about the way he or she was poised that made him uneasy. But before he could make up his mind whether to intervene, the wraithlike figure stepped off the path and slid slowly and silently into the water. It wasn't very deep, but as the cloak billowed out until only the head was visible, Harry realized that this was no eccentic jape, but someone in deep despair.

His own problems forgotten, he ran forward and was just in time to seize hold of the cloak, which came away in his hand. The hood fell back to reveal a tumbled mass of silver-fair hair which, even as recognition dawned in him, became pink-tinged with the sun's first rays.

"M-miss Devine! M-my dear young lady! Oh, dear God, you m-mustn't . . ." Not for the first time he cursed his disability as he struggled to keep her afloat one-handed. Her sodden cloak was growing heavier with every moment, dragging her down until the water washed over her face and she began to cough and splutter.

"No, no . . . Oh, please let me go!" she sobbed. "It is the only way out for me now!"

"Indeed I will not! Nothing can be that bad." But the weight of the water was increasing by the minute, and he wasn't sure how long he could support her, let alone haul her out. In an agony of frustration he looked about him, for surely there must be a rider somewhere taking the air. Most days when he wished to be alone, it was a wish that was seldom granted, but now when he desperately needed someone, the park was deserted. He redoubled his feeble efforts, and somehow by the grace of God managed at last to drag Isabella to the bank and deposit her, sprawling and choking, part on the verge, part still in the water, not daring to let go of her.

For a moment he lay, drawing in great gulps of air, before giving his attention to her once more and saw she was deathly white and shaking from head to foot. Cursing his clumsy efforts, he struggled in vain to remove her cloak, which was sodden, its ties in danger of choking her, and in so doing, was apalled to see the terrible bruises that disfigured her face and shoulders. He found that he was shaking, from rage as much as cold. He had seen terrible things on the field of battle, but who—or what—for surely no one even half-human—could do this to a delicate female. And then he remembered the rumors he had heard about her and von Schroder, and it suddenly became imperative that he should get her away from there and to a place of safety.

But how? He doubted whether she was fit to walk even a few steps, and in her sodden clothes she must already be chilled to the bone, for her teeth were chattering quite alarmingly. Perhaps, if he could support her as far as the Stanhope Gate, he might seek out Cressida Merriton. It was not all that far to Mount

Street, and of all the people he could think of, Cressida was by far the kindest and most practical of young ladies. She was also, or so he had heard, an early riser.

"Do you think you could w-walk if I help you?" he asked, as her breath became less rasping. "For you cannot stay here."

"Oh, no . . ." she moaned. "P-please—just leave me and go . . ."

Her despair filled him with a sudden terrible rage.

"That I will not." Few people among his London acquaintances had heard Harry speak with such force and without stammering once. "Come." He held out his hand. "I will not allow you to give up so easily. Nor will I permit anyone to harm you."

The note of authority in his voice penetrated her misery. She took his hand, which was surprisingly strong, and stumbled unsteadily to her feet. As she swayed he released her hand and put his arm around her, alarmed by her shivering as the sheer volume of water in her cloak weighed her down. "You will have to help me get this wretched thing off for a start," he said abruptly.

Too tired to argue, her shaking fingers struggled to release the ties. The cloak fell to the ground, exposing a thin gown that clung so revealingly to her shivering body that she might as well have been naked.

"Oh, good God! Here," he muttered, shrugging off his own greatcoat. "Take this. It is sodden at the bottom, but at least it's dry where it matters."

"I don't want . . ."

"Yes you do." The authority in his voice had the desired effect and she helped him to drape it round her shoulders. "Now, walk," he commanded with that same authority.

"I c-can't."

"Yes, you can. One step at a time."

God knows what we must look like, he thought, as they made slow and painful progress. But every movement, agonizing though it must be for the stricken girl, would at least get her blood circulating a little.

They were within sight of the Stanhope Gate when Isabella stumbled and began to sob that she could go no further.

"It isn't far now," Harry urged her, close to despair and exhaustion himself.

"I c-can't! Just leave me . . ."

"That I will not. Not after we've come this far . . ."

In desperation Harry looked around for a bench, and as he did so two riders entered the park. Cressida's white horse was immediately recognizable, and when the other proved to be Langley, he could hardly believe his luck.

"Cressida—Langley—over here!"

Within moments Alastair, his face grim, was out of his saddle and had relieved Harry of his burden, gathering Isabella into his arms, greatcoat and all, as if she were feather-light. She looked so still, so lifeless that Cressida's heart turned over with pity and not a little guilt. Poor, silly girl—how desperate she must have been—and how terribly alone. If only I had made more effort to foster a friendship with her, I might have saved her from so drastic a course of action.

"I was on m-my way to Mount Street," Harry gasped.

"Very sensible," Cressida said.

"Nearest place I could think of, though I doubt w-we'd have made it. I'm so damnably useless and as for Isabella—she seems to have given up all will to live . . ." He seemed to be struggling to contain an anger which finally burst forth. "I don't mind telling you, I have never felt so helpless in all my life!"

She felt a great wave of pity, but only said bracingly, "Nonsense. You have saved Isabella's life, which is no small thing. And once we get her home and dry, we shall soon make her more comfortable," Cressida said calmly, though privately, she was alarmed by the girl's pallor. "She will need a physician, of course. I only know of one—Dr. Grantly, who attends Lady Kilbride, and I cannot say he impressed me . . ."

"Grantly's an old woman," Alastair said over his shoulder. "Makes a fortune selling bottles of sweet colored water to gullible ladies like Aunt Beatrice as a cure-all. But I know an excellent physician who will do all that is possible for Isabella, and if von Schroder is mad enough to try looking for her, Isabella will be much safer at Langley House. You had better come along, too, Harry. You'll need a change of clothes."

Cressida was beginning to feel aggrieved at the way he had taken such complete charge, though she acknowledged that he had a point with regard to von Schroder. His temper was such that he might attempt almost anything if thwarted. But even if he discovered where Isabella was, he would surely not be mad enough to try and force his way into Langley House, and if he did, he would not get beyond the gates.

"I'll follow you shortly. I must let your aunt know what has happened, and collect a number of things that Isabella will need, not least of which will be a plentiful supply of nightgowns if she develops a high fever, as I fear she must."

"Of course. You are, as ever, practical," he said, but she could tell his mind was already elsewhere, and one didn't need to look far to discover the direction of his thoughts.

It is as though I have suddenly ceased to exist, Cressida thought. And wondered why she should feel so bereft.

Chapter Thirteen

Isabella's condition was soon giving grave cause for concern.

Alastair's physician friend, Dr. Reilly, whom she had been prepared to dislike on principle, had disarmed her within moments of meeting him. He was everything Alastair had said of him—a fine-looking black-haired Irishman with the bluest eyes she had ever seen, a smile that would charm the hardest heart, and, as Cressida soon discovered, a remarkably keen mind. The room was very quiet, the only sound being the painful rasping sound as Isabella fought for breath. After a thorough examination, which he had been pleased for her to attend, the doctor had shaken his head.

"The poor wee thing. I see so many like her—undernourished, inadequately clothed—some even damping their dresses to attract attention, more concerned with conforming to fashion than keeping body and soul together, much of which would seem to be apparent in in this young lady's case. Alastair has told me something of her history, which would seem to confirm my diagnosis. In fact, from the look of her I would say she has been starving herself repeatedly over a long period."

"That would certainly fit with what little I know of her," Cressida said. "Oh, the silly girl!"

"Quite. However that alone would not account for her present condition. As I believe you also suspected,

there is a more sinister element to be considered. I
have discovered two small fractures in her wrist, and
there is also a disturbing amount of bruising about her
body consistent with more than one severe
beating . . ." He drew aside the nightgown for Cressida
to see.

"Oh, poor Isabella! I knew the count had a bad
reputation. He was in Lisbon when I was there, and
there were plenty of rumors, though we never knew
how many were true. I did try to warn Isabella, but I
could and should have done more."

"Don't be blaming yourself, now, for I doubt she
would have listened. Some young women are natural
victims who seem to be drawn to that kind of man—
and from what Alastair has told me, this poor girl
would seem to be one of them. As for her injuries,
distressing though they appear, they will respond to
treatment, and given time should heal and leave little
in the way of scarring. The same may be said for her
general condition. With care and a sensible diet, there
is no reason why she should not make a full recovery"—he paused—"always assuming that the young
lady has the necessary will and determination to help
herself. But the attempted drowning would seem to
suggest that she may not wish to recover."

Cressida forced herself to take in every detail of the
bloodless face where the bruises stood out lividly, and
was filled with a sudden overwhelming sense of guilt,
all too aware that she had from the first dismissed
Isabella as a rather vain silly creature, only interested
in securing the attentions of a rich protector, and that
being the case, she had not therefore tried as hard as
she might to warn her of von Schroder's less-than-
salubrious reputation. Common sense had seemed to
suggest that any such warning would have been rejected out of hand, but that in no way assuaged the
helpless anger that now filled her.

"I fear that you may be right. But there has to be something you can do."

"Cases like this are never easy, but I assure you that all that can be done, will be done."

"I'm sure they will. Forgive me, I didn't mean to imply . . ."

"Of course you didn't," Dr. Reilly said with a reassuring smile, "for I'd know you for a young woman of sense even if Alastair hadn't assured me that you were entirely to be trusted."

"Alastair said that?"

"In so many words. And that being the case, I'll be frank with you. It's too early to make a prognosis, but from what little I know of her background and the absence of any immediate family, my greatest concern is that your friend may not attempt to fight against her condition," he said, shaking his head. "I can prescribe any one of several physics, of course, and she will have the best nursing available, but I fear there is no medicine guaranteed to cure a mind riven with despair. However, everything that can be done will be done. Nurse Hudson will be here directly. She is a motherly soul and I hope she will be able to encourage the young lady to take some nourishment. What she really needs, of course, is for someone to give her a reason to live."

It seemed a vain hope, but Cressida refrained from saying so, confining herself to practicalities.

"If your nurse needs any help, my maid, Jane Batty, is also an excellent creature. I could not, by any stretch of the imagination, call Jane motherly, but many a time in impossible situations I have seen her nurse people back to health when their case had seemed hopeless. And, of course, I shall be here quite often myself. A familiar face or voice may help to draw her back from the abyss."

Dr. Reilly gave her a quizzical look. "You are obviously a young lady of many parts. Who knows? Between us, we may yet save this poor troubled soul."

It was very quiet when he left to make his report to Alastair, the only sound being the rasping in Isabella's chest as she fought for breath.

Cressida had resolved to stay until Nurse Hudson arrived. From her admittedly limited experience of women calling themselves nurses, she had no great expectation of this one being any better, but in the event she was pleasantly surprised, for Nurse Hudson proved to be a comfortable, homely body whose keen eyes missed little, and who, once she had ascertained that Cressida posed no threat to her authority, was disposed to accept her frequent visits to the sickroom.

"Though I could wish I had better news for you, ma'am," she said on the second day. "She has stopped spewin' up that nasty water what she swallowed, which is something, I suppose. But as for takin' any proper nourishment—the times 'is lordship's had good tasty broth sent up from the kitchen—an' not a drop will she let past her lips . . ."

"Still, we must persevere."

Alastair would not have been pleased to hear Cressida including herself in the bid to save Isabella. She had already been accosted by him on her way up to the suite of rooms set aside for Isabella on the following morning.

"I do hope," he said with some asperity, "that you are not intending to make a habit of superintending the sickroom to the detriment of your many engagements. You were here until late last evening, and my aunt was not best pleased that you spoke of crying off your visit to Almack's tomorrow evening."

"Goodness! I had not supposed Lady Bea would mind. As for me—I can assure you that forgoing a ball or two is no great sacrifice. And I'm sure there will be many other opportunities to sample the delights of Almack's."

"Perhaps," he said austerely. "But there is no certainty about that. Aunt Beatrice has already assured Lady Jersey that you will be there. She and the other patronesses do not distribute their vouchers lightly and you offend them at your peril."

"Oh, come, Alastair! If they are so petty as to take offence at the merest trifle, I'm not at all sure I wish to go."

"It may seem a trifling to you, but it means a lot to my aunt that you should be accepted by the people who matter. Also, you should not need reminding that it was your persistence which brought about her transformation—and I, for one, would think very ill of you if you now mean to let her down by declining to attend Almack's as arranged, for it is she who will feel the brunt of any slight on the part of the Lady Patronesess—their displeasure might even drive her back into her old reclusive ways—and for what? So that you may spend your time playing nursemaid to someone whom you scarcely know, and who is already in capable hands."

It was a decided rebuke, and for a moment Cressida felt her throat constrict with angry unshed tears. He had been in an impossible mood since the previous evening, when, as soon as Dr. Reilly left, he had driven to the Pulteney to confront von Schroder, only to find that his quarry had already flown. She had felt immensely relieved, for a duel would have been the inevitable outcome, and the count was renowned for his ruthlessness in disposing of anyone who came up against him.

If he only knew how bitterly she blamed herself for what had befallen Isabella. Knowing the count as she did, she should have given the girl a stronger warning, though there was no guarantee that Isabella would have heeded the warning.

With this thought uppermost, she swallowed the protest that rose to her lips and drew a deep breath.

"You are quite right, of course," she said huskily. "I have neglected Lady Bea quite shockingly. It was just—oh, I can't explain, and if I could, you probably wouldn't understand. But I am sure that Nurse Hudson is more than capable, and Jane can always lend a hand, if needed."

A short while later Lady Beatrice was dozing in her chair when the sound of the doorbell jolted her wide-awake. She heard Martha's inevitable grumbling, followed almost immediately by Cressida's voice and her quick light step across the hall. A great wave of relief suffused her.

"I am sorry to have been away so long, dear ma'am. You must have been wondering where I had got to." Cressida bent to kiss her cheek. "I very much wished to have a word with Dr. Reilly about Isabella. He feels she may now be out of immediate danger, though her mental state still gives much cause for concern."

"Well, at least that must be considered progress of a kind," Lady Kilbride said, thinking that the whole business was, to say the least, a trifle odd. To be sure, it was laudable that Cressida should be so concerned, especially when one considered that she knew Miss Devine but slightly. But as for the rest—the way Alastair had taken the young woman into his home—to say nothing of engaging a doctor whose reputation was second to none, and was known to be shockingly expensive. Such a degree of consideration was decidedly odd, and would seem to suggest that the young woman was no stranger to him. She supposed she ought not to be surprised. Alastair was, after all, no better or worse than most young gentlemen in that respect, though of late she had hoped that he and Cressida might come to see one another in a more intimate light. To be sure, they had seemed to be on more agreeable terms. A small sigh escaped her.

"Well, I am very glad that the poor girl is improving," she said to Cressida, "especially if it means that you will not feel you have to be spending so much time at her bedside. I am sure the atmosphere cannot be healthy, and it isn't even as though she is a particular friend."

Cressida flinched, for her godmother's words only served to remind her yet again that had she been more of a friend to Isabella, she might have been able to prevent this tragedy. And she would not now be so consumed with the guilt of remembering the many times when she had suspected that the young girl was being ill-used, and had done nothing.

In the end it was Harry who brought matters to a head. He called the following afternoon just as Cressida was coming down the stairs after a brief visit.

"I w-will not stay above a m-moment," he said, flushing painfully. "Just w-wondered how Miss Devine goes on."

"Not too well, I'm afraid," Cressida said with a sigh. "Dr. Reilly says there is little more he can do. Since Isabella shows no sign of wishing to help herself, he is forced to conclude that she lacks the will to live."

"But that is terrible!" He was unusually flushed with agitation. "She is too young—too b-beautiful to throw her life away!"

"I couldn't agree more," Cressida said. "I promise you we have tried everything, but it is as though she has shut her mind to any form of persuasion."

Harry's face took on a look she had never seen before. And she saw at once how he must have been before the loss of his arm curtailed his exploits. His whole bearing had an air of authority and determination as he walked across to the bed, sat beside Isabella, and took hold of her hand.

"I know you can hear me, Miss Devine," he said, "so it is useless to pretend otherwise. I also know exactly what you are thinking—that if only you could die, all your problems would be solved. I know, because I, too, have been to the brink—looked into the abyss, and thought those very same thoughts. When I lost my arm, it seemed to me that death was preferable to a life destined to be forever curtailed by an obscene, useless stump."

Cressida listened in amazement. Not for the first time she noticed that when moved by powerful emotions, his stammer was almost nonexistent. And his voice took on an authority that could not be ignored.

"And you may be thinking, as I did then, that dying would be easier than waking each day to misery. But I have seen many men die, my dear young lady, and I can tell you that it is never easy. Once you can accept that, life again becomes a challenge."

In the silence that followed it seemed that they all held their breath. Then Isabella's face crumpled, she uttered a painful sob, and two large tears squeezed out and ran down her cheeks. And, as if released from some inner torment, the sob became a storm of weeping that wracked her whole body.

"Oh, my dear!" Cressida crossed swiftly to the bed and took Isabella in her arms, rocking her as she might a baby.

Harry slumped back in his chair, pale and exhausted. "I'm sorry. Maybe I shouldn't have . . . too drastic, but it s-seemed the only way . . . and it worked for me."

"No. You were right, I'm sure," Cressida said as she continued to cradle the sobbing girl. "It was exactly what was needed, but I would never have been brave enough to chance it."

It was thus that Alastair found them moments later. He stood for a moment taking in the extraordinary tableau. Then, "Would one of you tell me what the devil is going on?" he demanded with ominous quiet. "And where is Nurse Hudson?"

Harry tried to explain, but embarrasment caused his

stammer to return with painful frequency, so that Cressida swiftly came to his rescue.

"Nurse is, I hope, taking a well-earned break. And Harry has just performed a small miracle for which I declare we must all owe him a great debt of gratitude," she declared, explaining what had happened. "There is a long way to go, of course, but I am confident that the worst is now over and that in time and with careful nursing, Isabella should make a full recovery."

Chapter Fourteen

Cressida had taken particular care with her toilette for her visit to Almack's, having gathered from Lady Bea that nothing too unconventional should be contemplated. Madame Fanchon had, as usual, excelled herself, knowing exactly what was needed. She had designed for her a crepe gown in her favorite pale green with a bell skirt, tiny puffed sleeves, and a discreet neckline edged with tiny seed pearls.

Cressida had heard a great number of anecdotes about Almack's from so many different people that she hardly knew what to expect of the famous Assembly Rooms in King Street, presided over by its seven patronesses, ladies of distinction, whose smiles or frowns, according to Lady Bea, held the power to consign one to happiness or despair. Her godmother had been quick to add with a certain air of pride that without one of their much-sought-after vouchers, admittance to the Wednesday subscription balls was doomed to remain an impossible dream. Cressida would have been more than happy to remain one of the excluded, were it not for a wicked little worm of curiosity that demanded satisfaction by confirming that she owed her own good fortune, if one could indeed call it that, to not one, but two happy coincidences. As the goddaughter of Lady Kilbride she was already looked upon with favor. But she was convinced that the added cachet of being blessed with a father who had not only distinguished himself in the recent conflict, but was known to be intimate with the duke of Wellington, had clinched matters.

Certainly the patronesses, who were there in force, had greeted her with more cordiality than she had expected. Lady Cowper, Lady Jersey, and dear Lady Sefton, she already knew and liked, though Lady Jersey talked incessantly. And of the others, Princess Esterhazy was much the most approachable. Lady Castlereagh and Mrs. Drummond-Burrell were very grand, and Countess Lieven, she had met but once, and had found her much too haughty and not a little conniving. Pa, who could read women better than anyone she knew, had once called her a devilish mistress of intrigue. And no one could be held to be a more astute assessor of women than Pa.

However, Lady Bea had for so long been singing the praises of Almack's that Cressida was curious to see the exclusive Assembly Rooms in St James's for herself, though it was almost inevitable that they would prove a sad disappointment. And so they proved to be, especially when compared with the many beautiful ballrooms that had abounded in Lisbon, to say nothing of the splendid one at Langley House.

"Naturally I would not dream of admitting as much to my godmother," she confided to Perry when, just prior to supper, he solicited her for a waltz, which had only recently and somewhat reluctantly been accepted by the patronesses. "She cherishes the notion that Almack's is but one step removed from Carlton House, and is clearly enjoying every moment, so I would not have her disillusioned for the world."

"Very wise," murmured Perry, executing a graceful turn. "However, should her expectations stretch to the prospect of an equally elegant buffet, I feel I must also warn you that the refreshments, as with all else, leave much to be desired. The best one may hope for is bread and butter and stale cake—and to drink, nothing stronger than lemonade or tea."

"Oh, surely not!" Cressida wrinkled her nose in mock disgust. "You may think to bamboozle me, but I am more than five, you know."

"On my honor as a gentleman."

"But why then are people so eager to gain admittance?"

"Quite simply," he murmured, his gentle humor beguiling her, "because one has only to make something inaccessible to immediately render it desirable. You would not believe how it adds to one's social stature to be able to let fall in casual conversation that one has spent the previous evening at Almack's. And should you be able to add that one or more of the august patronesses had deigned to exchange as many as two words with you, your credit will immediately soar."

"Oh, really, that is absurd!"

"Quite. But then so much of life is absurd. You must surely find it so?"

It was impossible to take him seriously. "Frequently," she agreed. "Though I supposed it was I who was out of step with English customs, for in many ways, Lisbon hostesses observed a much stricter attitude toward young unmarried women than people do here, and but for Pa's insistence that I should accompany him to certain functions, my life would have been uncomfortably confined. As it was, I was permitted a degree of licence not accorded to others."

"I cannot imagine anyone confining you for long." Perry's gentle whimsical smile spoke volumes.

"Nor can I," she confessed. "I suppose it comes of having led a somewhat unconventional life. But all good things run their course eventually, and sooner or later I must resign myself to a more ordered existence."

Perry chuckled. "That will be the day. I shall await it with interest."

It was quite late in the evening when Cressida saw Alastair at the far end of the room, looking the very picture of elegance, and clinging to his arm with a degree of intimacy that was positively blush-making, was Lady Sherbourne, wearing a diaphanous gown of palest pink that revealed rather more than might be considered decent by the high sticklers among the patronesses.

Of Pa there was no sign, but then, as far as she was aware, he had been assigned to accompany the duke of Wellington on some diplomatic mission. It was unfortunate timing, for no sooner was he out of sight than Lady Sherbourne seemed almost blatantly bent on pursuing Alastair again. How could she? And how could he succumb so easily, remembering the pain she had caused him when he was so young and vulnerable? The momentary sensation of outrage that assailed Cressida was out of all proportion to this present situation, which could have any one of several quite rational explanations. Even so, if poor Lady Bea were to see them together, it might well bring on an attack of her palpitations, which of late she had all but overcome. Oh, how could Alastair be so insensitive when he must have known that his aunt was to be here this evening? She searched the groups of gossiping ladies and saw that her godmother was very much absorbed in conversation with Mrs. Arlington. Obviously she had not yet been made aware of Lady Sherbourne's presence, but for how much longer would she remain in blissful ignorance? If she did not see the said lady for herself, clinging so possessively to Alastair, sooner or later someone was bound to enlighten her.

It was clear that the situation was desperate, and would require desperate measures. She made her way across the room between dances and tapped Alastair's arm with her folded fan. "So you are here at last," she declared, summoning a coy smile that required every ounce of determination she possessed. "Your aunt has been looking for you this hour past. In fact, we had almost given you up for lost." She turned to his companion. "Gentlemen can be so unthinking at times, don't you agree, Lady Sherbourne?" With a conspiratorial smile she added, "I am sure you must frequently find my father one of the greatest culprits in that respect. He is incomparable as a negotiator, of course, and as such is much sought after, but he is also quite incorrigible. Poor Mama loved him dearly, but even she was occasionally moved to complain that he was never happier than when he was called upon to perform some delicate mission. He would be away in a trice, and hardly a word would she hear from him until the day he returned, laden with extravagant presents and vowing he had missed her desperately. But that is Pa all over."

Lady Sherbourne's expression did not alter perceptibly, although Cressida, being on the lookout for the least sign, was almost certain that she detected a faint tightening of the mouth.

"You surprise me, Miss Merriton, for I have never found him to be anything other than considerate as well as caring," she declared with a cloying sweetness. "But then I perfectly understand that he has many important duties to perform, and that when the duke has need of him, I must take second place. And I am so fortunate, for Alastair is taking wonderful care of me." She glanced up at him coyly. "We are such old friends."

"So I understand, Lady Sherbourne." It was a little like fencing, but with words in place of swords.

"Oh, please," she begged prettily, "you must call me Alice. And I will call you Cressida, if I may. It is ridiculous for us to be so formal in the circumstances, don't you agree?"

Alastair could hardly have failed to overhear their

conversation, though it was impossible to discern from his expression how he much he had read into Alice's coy, though wildly erroneous, version of their previous relationship. Or indeed, whether he had stopped to consider how Lady Kilbride might react upon being obliged to witness the apparent revival of a relationship that had once caused them both so much grief. He did however go so far as to put up his glass to scan the far end of the room, and when he finally spoke, his voice appeared untroubled.

"My aunt seems well content at present."

"Well, of course she is," Cressida retorted. "But that is not to say that she wouldn't be more than happy to see you, and be seen with you, for you know how proud of you she is. I have been obliged to reassure her more than once that you would come, though I had begun to wonder whether Isabella had taken a turn for the worse."

He flushed as if stung by her implied criticism. "On the contrary, she is making excellent progress, due in no small measure to young Harry who certainly seems to be spending a great deal of time with her. At least, that is Reilly's theory, and he should know."

There was almost a hint of pique in his voice. And with a perverseness that was not entirely in character, she was moved to say lightly, "Well, I daresay the good doctor may be right for in some ways the two have much in common. Both are virtually alone in the world, and both have been cruelly used by Fate. Perhaps you will think me overoptimistic, but I have recently begun to cherish the hope that each may have something to give to the other, and that they may in time form a more lasting relationship."

"Good God!" he said. "Does the female mind dwell on nothing else? Heaven defend me from matchmakers!"

"Oh, how unjust," she exclaimed, taken aback by his vehemence, which seemed quite out of proportion to a perfectly innocent observation. Surely he could not be jealous? "And your plea to the Almighty is quite unjustified, for I assure you that I abhor match-making practices quite as much as you do and would never presume to interfere in any way. But that does not preclude one from nurturing a kind of hope that two people who have suffered misfortune may eventually find happiness and a kind of healing in each other's company." She turned to Lady Sherbourne. "Would you not agree, my lady?"

"Since Alice has never, to my knowledge, met either party, she can hardly be expected to give an opinion," Alastair said abruptly.

Every instinct urged Cressida to take issue with him, but Perry arrived before she could do so. The usual pleasantries were exchanged, and as the sets were about to form for a quadrille, he enquired with his usual diffident charm whether, if Lady Sherbourne was not already spoken for, she might consider doing him the honor of partnering him.

Her eyelashes fluttered as she attempted, not entirely successfully, to look demure.

"I would be delighted, Mr. Devenham, if Alastair would not mind." She lifted her gaze almost coyly to Alastair, who gave his assent with an abruptness that led Cressida to question whether it arose from annoyance, or merely a reluctance to be left alone with her. Her question seemed to be answered almost at once.

"Would you care to dance?" he asked abruptly.

"Not if you mean to be ill-tempered."

"I am seldom, if ever, ill-tempered," he retorted in clipped tones.

"Oh, Alastair!" Her own lips quivered as she regarded the taut lines of his mouth. "Next you will be trying to convince me that you don't tell bouncers!"

He didn't answer, and for a moment she thought she had made bad worse. Then a reluctant smile tugged at the corner of his mouth. "Has anyone ever attempted to strangle you?"

Cressida chuckled softly. "Not as yet. Though I have been threatened once or twice. Which is most unjust, for I am in general the most amiable and conciliatory of creatures and have never knowingly harmed anyone."

At this he laughed and offered his hand. "Pax," he said. "And unless you especially wish to dance, suppose we go and see how Aunt Beatrice is enjoying her evening."

"An excellent idea," she said, putting her hand in his, and finding the firmness of his grasp strangely unsettling.

They discovered her ladyship looking slightly flushed, though with pleasure rather than distress. She was, she informed them, enjoying her evening enormously, and had scarcely had a minute to herself. Indeed she had spent most of the evening conversing with people she hadn't seen for years. "All the patronesses have been so kind. And Tilly is here, too, with Celia who has recently made her come-out. She has been away, you know—Tilly, that is. Her father—so unfortunate. He fell from his horse, and has a broken leg. She says he is very bad-tempered and consequently has been a great trial to her mother. However, all danger is now past and she has been able to return home, which is excellent news, for I have missed her."

"I am so glad, dear ma'am," Cressida said. "But you will let me know when you are beginning to feel tired. I would not have you overtiring yourself."

"Oh, don't worry about me. The evening is still young, and I am more than content to watch the dancers, though I forgot to bring my spectacles, so all is a trifle blurred—but very pretty nonetheless. Which reminds me, Alastair—I am told that Mr. Devenham has been very attentive with regard to dear Cressida, but I hope you mean to emulate him."

Alastair cast a wary glance at his companion. "*Mea culpa*, dear Aunt Beatrice," he said. "I was late arriving, since when, as far as I could tell, Cressida has scarcely been off her feet. However, if she has a dance to spare, I would be more than happy to oblige," he said dryly, and was not displeased to see her blush.

"You need not regard your aunt's heavy hints," she was quick to assure him when they finally moved away. "I perfectly understand that your attentions are much sought after elsewhere."

He shot her a look, unsure whether there was more to her remark than mere politeness. But if sarcasm was intended, there was no obvious sign of it in the eyes uplifted to him. They were soft green pools of light beneath the candelabra, without a trace of ill feeling in their glowing depths. If anything, they seemed to exude a warmth that, just for a moment, made his pulse quicken.

"Not to the exclusion of all else," he said with a certainty that surprised him almost as much as it did Cressida. "In fact, I should very much like to dance with you."

"Oh." For a moment her heart leapt and she was bereft of speech. "Then—yes, I would like it also. But a little later, perhaps. Alice will be expecting you to dance with her again. It is to be hoped your aunt does not recognize her." He uttered a soft expletive, but she persevered. "She knows, of course, about Alice and Pa, but still cannot overcome her distress at Alice's treatment of you."

"Good God, that was years ago!"

His manner changed abruptly, and she immediately cursed her too ready tongue. "I know," she said swiftly, in an attempt to put matters right, "and I have tried to persuade her to forget, but she still feels the hurt of it." But she was too late. The damage was done. And the rapport that appeared to have grown between them had melted away. The promised dance did not materialize, nor did she expect it to. But the rest of the evening had to be got through. In the event, it came as something of a relief when some time later Tilly Arlington sought her out and murmured discreetly that she thought Lady Kilbride was tiring.

"Do not let her know I have told you," she murmured. "It does seem such a shame that you should be obliged to leave while the night is yet young. I would take her home myself were it not for Celia. She is enjoying herself so much, and young Lord Hetherington seems quite taken with her." Mrs. Arlington lowered her voice. "His grandfather is the duke of Telforth, you know—twenty thousand a year at least, so they say . . ."

"Please—don't give it another thought. I would not for the world risk blighting Celia's prospects," Cressida put in swiftly. "I have enjoyed myself, but I shan't in the least mind leaving whenever my godmother wishes."

She would, of course. But not quite in the way Mrs. Arlington meant.

Chapter Fifteen

"Vienna?" Lady Kilbride exclaimed. "What on earth has Vienna to do with anything?"

"Quite simply, my dear Bea," Sir Charles explained, looking for all the world as smug as a cat who had stolen the cream, "it has everything to do with bringing peace to Europe and beyond. The situation is so complex that a Congress of the principal nations involved is to be held there to resolve matters. Castlereagh will be our principal negotiator, of course, but knowing of my considerable expertise and experience in such matters he has done me the honour of requesting that I accompany him."

"Oh, Pa—that is wonderful!" Cressida exclaimed, moving swiftly to hug him. "An honour, indeed. And nobody deserves it more."

"Have a care, m'dear," he besought her, fending her off. "This cravat took me a positive age to fashion."

"Poseur," she chided him.

"My dear!" Lady Kilbride chided, shocked by her godchild's apparent lack of respect for her parent and his attire, however deserving she might privately think Cressida's criticism to be. However, Charles seemed to take it all in good part.

But that he should be going to Vienna, of all places! For to her Vienna meant only one thing—it was the city where that wretched Alice, now Lady Sherbourne, had taken up residence during her period of mourning. And no doubt it was a city she would be happy enough to revisit if Charles were to invite her to accompany him, as he most surely would.

Alice might even persuade him to stay on for a while when his business was concluded. Not, she told herself, that it would concern her if he did, for any such nonsensical thoughts had long since been confined to the past, where they belonged. But, even so . . .

"And how have things been with you while I've been away, m'dear?" Charles was enquiring of his daughter. "Still enjoying yourself here, are you? Daresay you've made a lot of new friends—been to lots of balls and routs and the like?"

"Yes indeed," Cressida replied, almost too quickly. "People have been most kind. In fact, I have more invitations than I can possibly fulfil."

"Splendid, I'm glad to hear it. Always knew you'd take." He paused, then added casually, "Pity in a way, though. I had thought of asking whether you might care to accompany me."

"To Vienna?" Cressida's heart missed a beat, then began to race.

"It was just an idea. Thought you might enjoy it, for I daresay it won't be all business. Sure to be no end of balls and all manner of other jollifications. However, since you're obviously having such a good time here . . ."

"Which indeed I am!" Cressida was quick to aver. And then, unable to contain herself, sighed. "Oh, but . . . Vienna!" She swung round to her godmother. "Would you mind? Would it be too awful of me?"

Lady Kilbride struggled to hide her dismay. Mind? Of course she would mind. She had become so used to having her godchild around that the thought of losing her, even for a short time, was depressing in the extreme. But how could she voice her wretchedness with the child's eyes shining like stars however much she struggled to quell her longing. She drew a deep breath.

"My dear Cressida, of course I should miss you. But I would be a great deal more unhappy if you were to deny yourself such a splendid opportunity on my account after all you have done for me . . ." Lady Kilbride endeavoured to inject a positive note into her voice. "For it is entirely due to you that I now have a life again, and I would think myself quite churlish if I were to deny you such a splendid opportunity. Besides, the time will soon pass, and, thanks to you, I now have so many friends to support me. Tilly is forever tempting me to accept invitations. And it is not as if you will be lost to me forever. Is that not so, Charles?"

"What?" He reclaimed his attention which had strayed, just in time to catch the gist of the conversation. "Great heavens, no. Not a chance of that happening." His eyes acquired a mischievous twinkle. "Why, I daresay we shall be back almost before you've had time to miss us what with all the gadding about you seem to be doing these days."

"Charles! You make me sound like some flighty young thing."

"Which would not be so far of the mark. And growing younger and more comely by the day."

Lady Kilbride could feel herself blushing—something she had not had cause to do for many a year. She was very much aware of Cressida, who was now eyeing them both with interest and not a little curiosity.

"What is more, you still blush as delightfully as you did at seventeen."

"Now you are being ridiculous!" But her ladyship's heart beat a little faster just the same, as she added hurriedly, "Now, for goodness sake let us get back to the matter in hand. If Cressida is to come with you, there is much to be done."

"No need to panic," he said with all the casual certainty of one who never troubled to consider others. "The arrangements aren't as yet finalised, so Cressida should have ample time to get herself organized, give her apologies for any outstanding invitations and the like. Only don't take too long about it, m'dear. If I know Castlereagh, once matters are put in hand, he'll not wish to hang about."

From that moment on, Cressida hardly had a moment to spare. Or so it seemed. There were new dresses to be ordered, though she vowed she already had more than enough.

"Nonsense, my dear," Lady Kilbride exclaimed. "One can never have too many. There will be a great deal of entertaining, I shouldn't wonder, and your father will not wish you to be forever appearing in the same gowns."

"As if that were likely," she told Celia Arlington when they met at a rout later that week. It had hardly been possible to hear oneself think let alone speak amid the crush of people, but eventually they had found a relatively quiet corner. "I already have more than any sensible person can possibly need."

"And such beautiful gowns—so elegant." Celia, who was at the romantical stage, sighed. "I shall never be elegant."

"Oh, but you are much prettier!"

She wrinkled her retrusse nose. "I would rather I had some of your poise. Mama vows it will come with time"—she sighed again—"but I'm not so sure."

"Young Hetherington seems to be quite impressed." Cressida watched Celia blush and smiled. "In fact, I'd go so far as to say he was decidedly smitten."

"Do you truly think so? I feel so . . . oh, I don't know . . . when you were my age did you ever feel awkward and embarrased when you met someone . . . a young gentleman you really liked?"

"Not really," Cressida confessed ruefully, feeling

about ninety. "But then I suppose mine was hardly a normal upbringing. Mama died when I was barely out of short skirts and Pa came to rely on me quite heavily, so I grew up rather quickly."

Celia looked horrified. "That must have been dreadful for you!"

"At first, perhaps. But there was little time to grieve, for Pa had need of me. He always reckoned I should have been a boy, and perhaps he was right, for I almost always see life as an adventure—and, if nothing else, life with him is never dull."

These words proved curiously prophetic as the days raced past until only a few remained and there was still so much to be done. Her godmother was bearing up wonderfully well, but Cressida wasn't deceived, for she knew what a wrench it would be for Lady Bea when the time came for her to leave.

"I daresay I shall be back almost before you have had time to miss me, dear ma'am," she said bracingly, over a light luncheon, having noticed that Lady Bea had scarcely touched her meal. "And if the invitations on the mantelpiece are anything to go by, you will have any number of friends to help you fill your days."

"People are so good," her godmother sighed. And then, seeing a slight furrow forming on Cressida's brow, she pulled herself together. "You must not mind my foolish megrims, my dear. I promise you I shall not fall into a decline. Indeed, it seems almost certain that I shall not be allowed to do so. Tilly already has so many invitations lined up for me."

"So I should hope. And only consider how much we shall have to tell one another when I return."

Most of the packing she had left to Jane Batty. "For you are so much better at it than I am," she said.

"That's true enough," the hard-pressed maid grumbled. "Took me best part of an hour to get the creases out of that brown twill walking dress—and it'll all have to be done again when we get to Vienna."

"Poor Jane, what a trial I am," Cressida said, half-teasing. "I daresay you would rather be attending to Miss Devine now she is so much better and gathering strength by the day."

Her teasing brought only a grunt and a muttered, "Proper milk and water miss, that one. Still, by all accounts, she's not had much of a life."

"No indeed. Which reminds me, I have been very lax in my visits of late. I must find time to go and see her before we leave."

"That young gen'leman as lost his arm still seems to be dancing attendance on her as often as not. An' I did hear talk of his lordship taking her for a drive in the park one afternoon, but it'll need to be a closed carriage, I'm thinkin', for she's still frail, an' jumpy as a jack-rabbit whenever leaving the house is mentioned."

The maid's words strengthened Cressida's resolution, and she decided that there was no time like the present. She would make her way to Langley House that very afternoon.

The sound of music met her ears almost as soon as she was admitted. The footman, who was by now well acquainted with her, advised her that his lordship and the young lady were up in the long gallery.

"And enjoying themselves, if I am not mistaken," she said.

"Will I show you up, miss?"

Cressida's first inclination was to turn tail and return another day, but instead found herself rearranging her lacy shawl and saying, "Thank you, Albert, but I believe I can find my way."

The sounds of laughter and music reached her as she mounted the curving stair and approached the long gallery, where she paused at the entrance to take in the scene.

Harry was endeavouring to pick out a tune, one-handed, on the spinet while Alastair and Isabella tried to fit their steps to some kind of measure, with a conspicuous lack of success, so that they invariably dissolved into hearty fits of laughter.

Cressida stood for a few moments, unnoticed, taking in the happy scene and feeling curiously left out.

Alastair finally looked up and saw her standing there, and experienced a swift rush of pleasure—and something more that made his heart race.

"Cressida! What a surprise!"

She collected her thoughts and her composure, which just for a moment had seemed to desert her. "A pleasant one, I trust?"

"How could you doubt it?" he replied, taking refuge in his usual urbanity. "And you come in the nick of time, for we are sadly lacking a musician."

He was teasing, of course, but nonetheless she felt a momentary hollowing deep inside that perhaps the only way he saw her was as a convenience, which she immediately dismissed as ridiculous. And then they were all greeting her, drawing her in.

"We are due to set sail in a few days, and I wished to see how the patient was progressing before I left," she explained, adding with genuine warmth, "I am delighted to find you in such good spirits, Isabella."

"Thank you," the young girl returned haltingly. She still looked too thin and pale, and although her recent exertions had brought a tinge of colour to her cheeks, they had also left her a little short of breath.

"You have been very kind—all of you . . ." She swallowed nervously and her lovely blue eyes were brilliant with sudden tears. "And I have been so foolish . . ."

"Enough of that talk," Alastair said abruptly. "The past is over and done with. And the sooner you forget it, the better."

"It w-will become easier with time." Harry's voice

was calm and reassuring, and slowly Isabella's gaze shifted from Alastair to him.

"Yes. I know it is only weakness . . ."

"Which w-will pass. You are getting stronger every day. Remember that, and the b-bad days won't seem so bad."

As Cressida watched him, it suddenly became blindingly clear that Harry was in love with Isabella. But, judging by the way the young girl, head uplifted, turned to look so intently at Alastair, she feared Harry might be doomed to love in vain, and unaccountably her own heart hollowed at the thought, and its implications.

"Well I think you have made splendid progress," Cressida said. "And Harry is right, my dear girl. Things can only get better. I shall expect to see a great improvement when I return."

"So you really are going," Isabella said a little wistfully. "We shall miss you. I shall miss you."

"It is kind of you to say so," Cressida said. "And I shall miss you all quite dreadfully. But I hope you will be far too busy enjoying yourself to notice I've gone. Which reminds me, I must be away. There is so much still to be done, and little enough time in which to do it."

"Have a s-splendid time in Vienna," Harry said.

"Thank you. I'm sure I shall."

"And don't stay away t-too long."

"I won't." Just for a moment she wished she wasn't going. Then common sense prevailed. "And I promise to write."

"I'll come downstairs with you," Alastair said abruptly.

"There is no need," she protested. "You were so clearly enjoying yourselves when I disturbed you. And Jane is waiting below."

Alastair did not immediately answer, but took her arm and propelled her towards the staircase. "In fact," he finally concluded, "I'll walk back to Aunt Bea's with you."

"Now you are being foolish in the extreme," she protested.

"Then, pray indulge me. You will, after all, be free of me soon enough."

There was a harshness in his voice that puzzled her, and at the same time made her blood race, for she had done nothing, said nothing to merit such a reaction. "That isn't fair! I have never expressed any wish to be free of you."

"No more you have," he agreed, taking her arm and moving towards the door. "Take no notice. I am just feeling blue-devilled."

The door was opened for them by a waiting footman. Alastair ushered her through, retaining a firm hold of her arm, with Jane following several paces behind. Had Harry's growing attachment to Isabella angered him—surely not? And if it had, what business was it of hers? Nevertheless, the thought brought depressingly little comfort.

And then, all too soon, it seemed, they had reached Mount Street. "You will come in to see Lady Bea?"

"I think not," he said. He was looking at her in the strangest way—as though he would memorize every feature. "I suppose there is no talking you out of this crazy venture?"

"It isn't crazy," she protested. "It will be a great experience, for I have long wished to see Vienna."

Cressida held her breath as for a moment he seemed on the verge of saying more. If only he would beg me to stay, she thought . . . it isn't too late, even now . . .

But already he was tipping his hat, making some clipped reference to a safe journey, striding away. And there were painful tears at the back of her throat as she watched him go.

Chapter Sixteen

Their arrival in Vienna was like entering another world.

After the inevitable boredom, cramped quarters, and restrictions of the ship that had carried them from England, to say nothing of the occasional storm, and the less-than-welcome company of Alice, who became more and more irritable as time went on, tempers all round had inevitably become frayed.

Alice seemed determined to monopolize Sir Charles at every available opportunity, which did little to soothe his irascibility. Cressida had felt duty-bound to explain that her father was invariably like a caged lion on board ship. But the warning fell on deaf ears, and Alice's incessant complaints about everything from the inclement weather to accusations that Charles was deliberately avoiding her was guaranteed to bring out the worst in him.

He had always been most at ease at such times with his own kind, and by a stroke of good fortune there were other, less senior members of the diplomatic service also travelling with them, eager young gentlemen of good families who were eager to further their careers by quizzing Sir Charles about the direction the forthcoming Congress might take, and in particular, its many possible conclusions.

When Alice realized that all of her well-tried ploys were doomed to failure, she attempted to engage in a little harmless flirtation with the more impressionable

of the young gentlemen, but most were wary of incurring
the great man's wrath, and the few who were tempted
were not really to her liking, and certainly not worth
the risk of making Sir Charles jealous. Though in that,
had she but known it, she would have been doomed to
disappointment, for his mind was on greater matters.

Cressida felt duty-bound to at least try to keep Alice
occupied, but her efforts were at best received with coolness, and mostly proved to be totally ineffective, so that
the sight of land had come as a blessed relief.

Her one consolation was the realization that, sooner
rather than later, her father was likely to find his latest
love more of a trial than a blessing. He had already
been moved to take her to task on more than one occasion when she had complained about his obsession with
Congress business. And there was still the prospect of
the long overland journey to Vienna to be endured in
the exceedingly cramped conditions of a coach, which
would try everyone's patience even more.

Sure enough, once they were on *terra firma,* her father,
being eager to reach Vienna as soon as possible, was not
disposed to linger. He commandeered two coaches, and
dispatched the young hopefuls of the party to make their
own way to Vienna in one, keeping the slightly larger
one for himself. In a very short space of time they were
on the road, and it soon became clear that he was not
about to linger any longer than was absolutely necessary
at each halt, even to please his beloved, who grew more
sullen with every hour that passed.

It did not help that she had no personal maid of
her own, which made her doubly resentful of Jane
Batty's presence. "I fail to see why she is allowed to
accompany you when your papa was quite adamant
that we could on no account bring my maid," she
declared peevishly on the first night when they finally
stopped at a small inn, and she discovered that she
was required to share a room with Cressida, Sir
Charles having declared that the beds were niggardly

at best—and the rooms scarcely wide enough to accommodate his own generous frame.

Alice had made no attempt to lower her voice, though she could not help but be aware that Jane was well within earshot. Mistress and maid exchanged glances.

"But then, you see, Pa doesn't regard Jane simply as a maid, for she is more like one of the family," Cressida replied with cold clarity. "Indeed, she has been with us for years, caring for us through thick and thin, so she is well used to travelling and always knows exactly what is needed and how to procure it. We would not be without her for an instant."

She said no more until Jane had left the room to procure a jug of hot water. Then she vented the full force of her anger upon Alice.

"Don't ever speak that way again of Jane in her hearing. I meant every word of what I said, and it is nobody's fault but your own if you are inconvenienced. No one forced you to make this journey. Pa would have understood perfectly if you had declined to come—in fact, to be brutally frank, I doubt if he will remember you are here at all once the Congress begins. And you certainly won't endear yourself to him by constantly finding fault when his temper is already on a short rein. I had supposed you might have realized by now that once his mind is set on something, nothing short of a full-scale barrage, or an act of God, will persuade him to alter course, and that any additional source of irritation will merely provoke him further and bring down on any hapless creature who gets in his way the full force of his wrath."

Alice gasped, and Cressida watched the beautiful face grow stormier by the second, so that eventually, for the sake of peace and quiet, she was moved to conclude with some reluctant semblance of sympathy, "However, I do appreciate that you are not used to travelling in this neck-or-nothing fashion, and that you will be missing your maid as well as most of your creature comforts. But we had little choice, for Lord Castlereagh needed Pa urgently. So, after some consideration I have decided that as long as Jane has no objection, and you promise to treat her kindly, you may within reason avail yourself of her services. When we reach Vienna, of course," she added with gentle malice, "you will doubtless be able to engage a maid who is more to your liking. I daresay they may be in short supply with so many people in need of their services, but you will undoubtedly be able to procure someone suitable through the kind offices of your many friends."

The atmosphere between them remained cool thereafter, and the generous offer of Jane's services was pointedly ignored. But all was forgotten when they finally reached the outskirts of Vienna through a series of tiny picturesque hamlets. She came to life, as a flower opens to the early rays of the sun, and was all conciliation.

"Won't be long now, m'dears," said Sir Charles, who was also restored to his usual genial self, for he was never one to hold lingering grudges. And as a further bend in the road was negotiated, he leaned forward. "Ah, there now—what did I tell you . . . isn't that a sight to behold."

"Oh, Pa!" Cressida exclaimed.

She had encountered many beautiful places in her travels, but none that could compare with the panorama of color and beauty spread out before her. Whichever way she looked, the views were breathtaking. There were huge beech trees fast turning to a deep glowing red in the autumn sunshine, and oak and maple, with here and there, catching the light, the silver shiver of aspens. And far beyond, rising like a huge dramatic backcloth, stood the tall black pines of the Wienerwald.

Then, almost before she had time to draw breath, Vienna itself came into view and there seemed to be a kind of magic in the air—something she had not felt anywhere else in her travels. Within moments they had entered the city, and she was lost in admiration of its beautiful and varied buildings.

"It is quite exquisite!" she murmured, and turned to Alice with more warmth than either had shown during the remainder of the journey. "And that wonderful park that we passed—the Prater, you called it. I have seen nothing to equal it. Oh, yes—I can quite see why you wished to come back."

Alice herself seemed strangely unmoved for someone who had so often proclaimed her attachment to this oft-acknowledged city of dreams, but Cressida was already far too absorbed to notice.

Sir Charles, with the forethought born of experience, had managed to procure the lease of an unusual, but delightfully ornate, house in a prestigious position quite close to the Hofburg, where the Emperor Francis was to play host to a formidable gathering of royal personages, including, or so she had heard, an emperor and his empress, four kings, one queen, two hereditary princes, three grand duchesses, and three princes of the blood. For most people the house would have more than sufficed. But Alice was not most people.

"It will do well enough, I daresay," she said, peering into each downstairs room with a distinct want of enthusiasm. "Though the woman who passes for a housekeeper leaves much to be desired. If only I had known we were to come here, I would not have sold my beautiful house in Am Hoff."

"Well, I think this house is quite charming in its quaint rococo fashion—the rooms are large and airy, and I'm sure I shall grow quite fond of those delightful plaster cherubs smiling down at us from the ceiling of the rear salon." Cressida chuckled. "And only consider what a talking point they will be when we entertain! As for the housekeeper, she seems willing enough. I have known many a worse one than Frau Helger, as Pa will readily confirm," Cressida declared, more in defense of her father than from any certainty of being right. He never liked being crossed at the best of times, and at present was looking less than impressed by Alice's patronizing remarks. Could it be, Cressida wondered, that he was beginning to see through her, to tire of her constant complaining, for all that he held his peace? Now, there was a thought.

However, there was little time to put her theory to the test, for Sir Charles was in demand almost from the moment they arrived. He missed supper, and arrived back very late, which did not please Alice. She had sulked throughout the evening, but all must have been forgiven, for she eventually floated down to breakfast the following day when the morning was half gone, dewy-eyed, and trailing her silky peach-bloom pegnoir, with her silver-fair hair undressed and floating loose to caress her shoulders. She was clearly prepared to be gracious, only to find Sir Charles long gone once more.

"Pa was sorry he had to leave so early," Cressida said, making a conscious effort to remain pleasant, and even feeling a little sorry for Alice as she rang for Frau Helger. "It is really too bad of him, and almost before we have had time to settle in, too. But a letter was delivered well before breakfast from Lord Castlereagh requesting Pa's presence at the earliest opportunity."

"How very inconsiderate of his lordship." The delightful lower lip pouted. "I had hoped to show Charles around Vienna a little."

No mention of me, Cressida noted, annoyance mingling with relief, for she had much rather explore by herself. "I daresay Lord Castlereagh is eager to discuss with him the form the Congress is likely to take as soon as possible. It is, after all," she concluded with a modicum of satisfaction, "why Pa has come here."

"And he will be in his element, of course," Alice said waspishly. "I suppose I may expect to see nothing of him until this evening, and think myself lucky to see him then." She toyed with a warm croissant, sipped black coffee, and sighed deeply. "I do hope this is not going to become a habit."

Cressida eyed her dispassionately. "If your expectations run to having Pa dancing attendance on you, then I fear you will hope in vain, and will be well served, for you must surely have known how it would be when you insisted on accompanying him."

"Of course I was aware that he would be in demand, but I had not expected to be abandoned so soon—on our very first morning."

"Then you don't know Pa as well as you thought, for intrigue, negotiation, anything of that nature is the very breath of life to him. And as for being abandoned." Cressida bit back her irritation. "That is surely a gross exaggeration, for you are hardly a stranger to Vienna, and must have friends here, and you also have me for company, should you need me— unless you consider my presence to be of no account."

"Don't be ridiculous! You are deliberately twisting my words!" Alice set her cup down with a clatter, her face flushed with anger. "This coffee is cold. Ring the bell for that woman who is supposed to be the *housfrau*. She is obviously incompetent."

Her patience at an end, Cressida pushed back her chair and stood up. "I am not here to wait on you. I have only stayed this long out of politeness, in the hope that you might put in an appearance. If you want fresh coffee, you may ring for it yourself. But I must warn you that Pa will be less than pleased if you alienate Frau Helger before we have been here five minutes. I imagine housekeepers are not easily come by with Vienna as crowded as it is. You may think you can twist Pa 'round your little finger, but he is every bit as self-centered as you are, so you could be in for a nasty surprise if you try him too far. As for me, I intend to go out."

She closed the door with a snap, leaving Alice openmouthed and bereft of speech, and went to her room to calm down. How could my father be so easily bamboozled by such a self-centered creature? she thought, pacing the floor. Men are such fools. But her temper, so easily roused by Alice, could seldom be sustained for long, and was almost dissipated by the time Jane came to tidy the room.

"I can come back later," the maid said gruffly.

"Don't be ridiculous. You are not dealing with Lady Sherbourne now."

"Been playin' the martyr again, has she?"

Cressida choked on a reluctant laugh. "Does it show that much?"

"Only to them as knows you."

"My own fault. I shouldn't let her get to me. But I am resolved to ignore her petty jibes from now on, as far as I possibly can. And once she has recovered from the journey, I hope she will be out a great deal, renewing old acquaintances."

"That'll be nice for them," said the maid dryly.

Cressida tried to look disapproving, but again her mouth curved irrepressibly up at the corners. "I hope so, for we might then see less of her. As for me, I mean to go out. There is so much to see and I can't wait to begin."

In no time at all she had donned her favorite bronze green pelisse, and its matching bonnet, and, having informed Frau Helger of her intentions, let herself out of the door, her spirits fully restored.

The day was fresh, the street was crowded, and there was a general air of expectancy. Cressida had picked up a smattering of most languages in her travels, and gradually discerned that some kind of procession was imminent. Amid the excited babble of the people around her, she eventually gathered that the Czar of Russia and his entourage was expected to pass by at any moment. She had seen the young czar briefly from a distance at Prinny's Carlton House celebrations and had then thought him benignly plump, and rather under his mother's thumb. But now, affected in spite of

herself by the enthusiasm of the throng, she decided to
join the fun. She had not long to wait before the unmistakable sound of hoofbeats and the jingle of harness
became discernible above the babble of the crowd.

Cressida had seen many processions in her young
life, but this cavalcade had an air about it that both
entranced and amused her, with the nodding of
plumes and sunlight glancing off gleaming cuirasses.
And at the head of the parade rode the young czar,
standing out amid the kaleidoscope of color—a vision
in dark green and gold, the padded tunic of his uniform, with its high gold collar and gilded epaulets,
smothered in lace, giving him the curious air of a well-
stuffed toy soldier. A part of her thought it all ridiculously theatrical, but in spite of that, one could not
but be affected by its sheer magnificence.

And as she watched, to her surprise and pleasure,
she saw a familiar figure at the czar's side—Prince
Metlin, for it was surely him. No one else could possibly possess such a handsome set of red-gold whiskers.
Oh, goodness, how the sight of him took one back.
He was exactly as she remembered him, if a trifle
stouter in his colonel's uniform. But then it must be all
of nine or ten years ago—before Lisbon had become
isolated by the vagaries of war. She had been little
more than a child, but even so, the prince had treated
her with the utmost gallantry, and she had fallen head-
long in love, though she was realistic enough even at
so young an age to know that her love would remain
unrequited, and she had been content to worship from
afar. But what fun it would be to meet him again.

Her spirits restored, Cressida spent an agreeable hour
or more wandering through the crowded streets and arrived back in a much-restored frame of mind to find that
her father had also returned. He seemed in remarkably
good fettle, and had already gone some way to restoring
Alice's spirits. The reason soon became apparent.

"Your papa is to take me to the opera house this

evening," she exclaimed with a gleam of triumph in her shining eyes. "Lord Castlereagh has presented him with tickets for the ballet. It is *Flora and Zephire* with Signorina Bitottini."

Sir Charles looked a little sheepishly at his daughter. "The thing is, m'dear, there are only two tickets. Seemingly, they are practically like gold dust."

"Oh goodness, Pa! Don't worry about me. I shall be well content to spend a quiet evening with a book. Life has been one long rush during the last few weeks. It will be a pleasure to put my feet up for a while."

Sir Charles gave her a searching look. "Feeling all right, are you, m'girl?"

"Yes, of course. Why should I not be?"

"No particular reason. Except that it's not like you to care so little at missing a visit to the theatre, let alone plead tiredness. Never took you for a book-worm, either."

"There are many things you don't know about me, I daresay," she said carelessly.

"I daresay there are. Even so . . ."

"Even so, nothing. I shall be quite content, I promise you. You may take Alice to the theatre with a clear conscience. We shall be inundated with invitations soon enough, I daresay."

"Well, if you are sure?"

"Of course she is sure, Charles." Alice's voice sounded sharp even in her own ears, and some inner caution warned her that it would not do to alienate him by criticizing his daughter. She forced a smile and said with ingratiating sweetness, "Cressida is not one to dissemble like some folk, are you, my dear?"

This comment, so innocently delivered, caused father and daughter to exchange a wry smile, though Alice could not for the life of her understand why. At such moments she felt curiously excluded—and felt an uncomfortable tightness in her throat.

"I had better go and tell Frau Helger that we would

like dinner early." Cressida stood up and walked to the door, aware of Alice's discomforture, and not wishing to add to it. "Oh, by the way, Pa—you'll never guess who I saw this afternoon when I went out for a walk. I was just in time to witness a perfectly splendid procession headed by the czar, and who should be beside him but Prince Metlin. He did not see me, of course, nor would I expect him to acknowledge me even if he had recognized me, for he was totally absorbed in his duties."

"Ah, yes." Sir Charles said, "I remember someone telling me that he is top of the trees these days—a colonel in the czar's own special troop, no less. The troop is more of a showpiece than an actual fighting unit, of course, not to be taken too seriously. But it's quite an accolade for Metlin, nonetheless." He chuckled. "I shall look forward to renewing our acquaintance. Bound to meet up with him sooner or later."

"Do you mean to say you are actually acquainted with Prince Metlin?"

Alice sounded decidedly peevish and not a little envious, which brought a smile to Cressida's lips.

"Yes, indeed. I once had the honor of receiving a proposal of marriage from him," she reminisced softly. The smile broadened as she noted Alice's look of disbelief. "Sadly, I was only eight years old at the time, so I could scarcely hold him to it, but I still treasure the memory." She chuckled. "In fact, I may well remind him of it when we meet, as we surely must."

There was a momentary flash of wild jealousy—or possibly something more dangerous than mere jealousy—mirrored in Alice's eyes. It was so brief that her father was clearly unaware of it. But Cressida saw it, and instantly realized that she must learn to guard her tongue when Alice was present. It was tempting to regard her as nothing more than an empty-headed schemer who craved power and position almost as much as wealth but just occasionally one glimpsed a darker side to her nature.

Chapter Seventeen

Almost before they had settled in, the invitations began to arrive.

"Goodness!" Cressida exclaimed. "At this rate we shall scarcely be an evening at home!"

"I should hope not, indeed." Alice surveyed the growing pile of cards with a satisfaction verging on smugness. Gone was the aura of discontent that had hung about her since their arrival—forgotten, her constant complaints that Sir Charles seemed to have forgotten her entirely—was never home.

"I suppose it is no more nor less than I should have expected," she confessed with an irritating coyness. "Your father is at the very hub of things after all, and must inevitably receive the attention due to him. And he will naturally rely on me to support him."

No mention of his daughter's support, Cressida fumed inwardly. But it was no more than could be expected of Alice. Her ennui quite forgotten, the only thing now on Alice's mind was that all her ambitions were about to be fulfilled.

"I shall need more gowns, of course. And a good hairdresser. There used to be an excellent *frisseur* in a quaint little street somewhere near Ball Gasse. He was wickedly expensive, as I remember, and will probably be even more so at present, but one cannot possibly regard such trifling matters. I must, after all, do your papa justice. It might be as well to make my way there this afternoon, for he is bound to be very much in demand."

Cressida did not trouble to reply, and Alice clearly did not expect her to do so. Like a child surrounded by all kinds of sweetmeats, she became totally absorbed in making lists of what she would need, or simply must have, without a thought for anyone else, until Cressida could have screamed. Finally, having done little more than pick at her luncheon, prepared with such care by Frau Helger, Alice pushed her plate aside and rose from the table, declaring that she could not be still a moment longer, and had resolved to visit a certain baroness who had been one of her greatest friends before her return to England, and who would be sure to know where to find the elusive hairdresser. "And we really must purchase something suitable in a carriage. I wonder your father has not considered it to be a first priority, except that these days he scarcely considers us at all. It is all diplomacy, diplomacy . . . I vow he thinks of nothing but all those tedious negotiations."

Which is why he has been sent here, Cressida longed to say, except that her words would have fallen on deaf ears. To argue would be fruitless, and in any case, it was difficult to feel sorry for anyone so totally selfish.

Alice made no attempt to invite Cressida to accompany her, which came as no great surprise, and had she done so, the invitation would have been politely but firmly declined.

The house was pleasantly peaceful when she had gone, and Cressida decided to sit down and write to Lady Bea.

Dear Godmother,
We are here at last and comfortably settled in a charming little house—too little, I think, for Alice's grandiose tastes, but I'm glad to say that Pa has

*resisted all her objections, and in any case, I doubt
there is a single unoccupied dwelling in the whole
of Vienna, so many people are assembled, and
who can blame them for it is the most beautiful
city you could possibly imagine—I do not have
words to describe it. And there is also a wonderful
park, which I cannot wait to explore. We see very
little of Pa, for Lord Castlereagh is already de-
manding much of his time, which does not please
"you know who." Almost all the principal partic-
pants are now here, and there is much cheering
whenever anyone of importance appears. But already there are objections to the proposed agenda,
Monsieur Talleyrand and Don Labrador of Spain
being the most recent offenders, and Pa fears that
an agreement suitable to all parties will not be easy
to reach. He also says that the emperor fears the
possibility of spies infiltrating the delegations, and
it is rumored that the head of the secret police will
have spies placed in all the embassies. There is
even talk of them going through the wastepaper
baskets of delegates, which is too silly for words
and surely cannot be true. Heigh-ho! On a lighter
note, the emperor has presented Prince Metternich
with the task of keeping us all amused, so we may
expect all kinds of diversions. Already we are invited to a great many balls and grand routs. I will
write again very soon to tell you about them.*

Your loving and devoted godchild, Cressida.

The letter completed, she was about to ask Frau
Helger how one set about sending it when the doorbell chimed. She opened the door of the salon slightly,
mystified as to who might be calling. The voice was
instantly recognizable, causing her heart to miss a
beat, and she instantly reproached herself for what
could only be regarded as the foolish reaction of a
green girl, and stepped into the hall.

"Your Highness," she said with commendable composure. "What a pleasant surprise. Do come in. My father is not here at present, but . . ."

Prince Metlin's tawny eyes twinkled with good humor. "But then it was not your father I came to seek, my dear young lady, charming fellow though he is," the prince confessed. "In fact, it was he who was so kind as to inform me that you were here, and I at once secured his gracious permission to invite you to take a drive with me to the Prater, if you have nothing more important to do."

"How wonderful—and how very strange, for I had this sudden longing to visit the Prater. Also, I have a letter to post to my godmother, and I am not sure how to go about it."

"Then it was clearly meant that I should visit you today," he said with that crooked smile she remembered so well.

Cressida found herself blushing. "Will you come into the salon while I get ready? I won't keep you more than a few minutes."

"There is no hurry. I have an enthusiastic young tiger who is content to mind my carriage. But what a charming room," he exclaimed, looking around as he stepped inside. "All those cherubs and acanthus leaves. So very . . . Viennese!"

"Aren't they, though?" She was surprised and quite ridiculously pleased to find that he shared her opinion. "Alice . . ." She found it quite impossible to explain who Alice was, and hoped he wouldn't enquire as she concluded briefly, ". . . she doesn't care for them, but I have quite fallen in love with them."

"Fortunate cherubs," he murmured, his eyes twinkling in a way that caused her heart to skip a beat.

Heavens! she thought, making her way hastily to her room. She had forgotten how very personable he was—how she had secretly fallen in love with him all those years ago. Oh, the pain of unrequited love when

one is eight years old! How she had suffered. Had he
known, she wondered. And if so, had he remembered?
Common sense told her that, if he had, he must also
have recognized it as being no more than a childish
infatuation. As for her, she had long since grown old
enough and wise enough to realize that the Prince
Metlins of this world were not to be taken seriously.

So it was a pleasantly composed Cressida who presently returned to the salon, charmingly dressed in a
splendid redingote of ivory twill, closed high at the
neck with a collar of ermine, and a matching toque
with a dashing little brim fashioned in the same color.

Prince Metlin's approval was unconfined as he led
her toward his carriage——an elegant phaeton entirely
lined with crimson velvet. "It is altogether clear to
me," he murmured, lifting a quizzical eyebrow, "that
the child who once danced for me like an angel, has
become a beautiful and most discerning young woman."

Her heart flipped, for although she knew flattery
came as easily to him as breathing, his words moved
her, nonetheless. Fearing that emotion might betray
her, she said lightly, "And the handsome prince who
applauded her efforts with such gallantry is as smooth-
tongued now as he was then."

He threw her a rueful glance and for a moment she
was afraid that she might have offended him. Then the
red-gold whiskers unmistakably twitched. "Not only
beautiful, but a great deal too discerning. However, I
refuse to be cast down. Once we have disposed of
your letter, we will enjoy each other's company in the
sylvan delights of the Prater."

And so they did. It was every bit as beautiful as she
had been led to believe. The sun had tempted a great
many people out, some on foot and others riding in
carriages or on horseback, so that the overall impression was of a constantly moving kaleidoscope of color.

"If this pleases you, then I know what will delight
you even more. If you permit me, when the weather

grows a little warmer, I shall arrange for a picnic in the woods above Vienna, and you may ask whomever you please."

"That would be wonderful," she exclaimed, turning to him with glowing face. And then, looking some way beyond him, she saw, travelling in the opposite direction, a very smart low-slung phaeton. But it was the two occupants who caused her to utter a stifled cry.

"My dear young lady, is something wrong?"

"Yes . . . no! That is to say . . . I don't know, but I rather fear there might be." She turned impulsively to the prince. "Are you by any chance acquainted with Count von Schroder?"

The prince did not reply immediately. When he did, his voice had a curiously neutral tone. "Why do you ask?"

"Because I believe him to be a villain of the worst kind, and I have just seen him driving past in the company of . . ." She hesitated, aware that she was in danger of being indiscreet. 'Of someone I know."

"Ah!" he said softly. "Then I share your concern, though it may be a perfectly innocent encounter."

"I doubt he knows the meaning of innocence. Except as a despoiler of so admirable a virtue." Involuntarily she shivered, though the sun was warm.

"You do not like him, I think," the prince murmured.

"I detest him," Cressida said with feeling. "And with good reason, for I have seen the harm he can inflict. The man is a monster; but like a snake he can also charm, and women seem to succumb, even when they sense danger."

Prince Metlin was silent for a moment. "One has heard rumors, of course."

She continued impulsively, "Somehow it had not occurred to me that he would be here, and yet, of course, I should have realized that Austria is his homeland, and since Alice lived here for several years, it is even possible that they might already be acquainted. Oh, this is the very devil!" she exclaimed, and then, with a wry smile, "Forgive my wretched tongue. Travelling for so long with my father as I did was fun, but I fear I picked up some very unladylike language . . ." She heard him chuckle. "However, it is unforgivable of me to foist my worries upon you."

"On the contrary, I am intrigued. Naturally, the count has friends at court, but not everyone admires him, and there have occasionally been rumors of an unsavory kind."

Cressida knew she ought not to tell tales, but this was no ordinary tittle-tattle, and so she related what she knew, finishing with what had befallen Isabella.

He was silent for a moment. "Your father knows nothing of all this?"

"Gracious, no. And I really don't think that I can tell him—or even give Alice a hint, for she will not believe me, and will only accuse me of jealousy. But hopefully, since she is older and more experienced than Isabella, she will be better able to take care of herself."

There was a small silence, and Cressida was suddenly plagued with guilt. It was not, after all, very commendable to tear someone's reputation to shreds in such a way, even someone as unscrupulous as von Schroder. She might well have put the prince in a difficult position.

"Oh, please—forget all I have said. I should not have spoken . . ."

"You feel strongly, one can tell."

Prince Metlin sounded sympathetic, if a trifle detached, and Cressida felt even more guilty. "No. And there is nothing I can, or indeed should, do—or say. That is the nub of the matter, is it not?"

"I fear so, dear young lady. Hopefully, the count will behave with some degree of discretion throughout the Congress, for, if nothing else, he will not wish to fall foul of Emperor Francis, who is so concerned that nothing should detract from his handling of events that he has his spies everywhere."

The remainder of the afternoon passed most agreeably, with the expectation of many more such occasions to be enjoyed.

Alice came home looking mightily pleased with herself, having accomplished all and more than she had set out to do. The hairdresser had been most accomodating once she had let slip Sir Charles's name, together with a hint or two concerning his closeness to the emperor. It was indeed fortunate, he had gushed, that the lady who should have come that very afternoon had been obliged to cancel—laid low by a sudden chill—so that, if she was not otherwise engaged, he could fit madame in there and then.

"As I suspected, he was monstrously expensive, but one cannot be counting pennies when one is dealing with an artist and he is almost a genius, wouldn't you say?" She twirled so that Cressida might admire his handiwork to the full.

"A genius indeed," Cressida was obliged to agree. She was, however, obliged to bite on her tongue as the older woman went on to relate her encounter with Count von Schroder, who was, she declared, the most intriguing of creatures. "We met briefly when I was living here before, though to some extent we moved in different circles." She fluttered her eyelids, looking coy. "But for some reason, he swears he remembers me, and I vow he exudes the kind of arrogant charm that carries with it a fascinating hint of danger . . ."

Alice seemed oblivious of her companion's unease as she continued to eulogise about the count, her pleasure only turning to discontent when she discovered that Cressida had been taking the air in even more illustrious company.

"Do, I beg of you, have a care, Alice," Cressida

said impulsively. "The count is a dangerous man, as I have reason to know."

"Well really! How dare you preach to me, my girl—for girl you are, and a green girl at that, for all that you flaunt your supposed experience. And just because you happen to be slightly acquainted with someone in an elevated position, does not give you sufficient experience to cast a slur on someone far above you in experience."

"I know that he half-killed at least one poor young woman who fell prey to his particular brand of brutal charm."

"Then she probably asked for it."

Anger mingled with indignation threatened to spill over into a positive tirade as the image of Isabella bruised, battered, and half-drowned returned to haunt Cressida once more. Only the knowledge that nothing would convince Alice she was not air-dreaming prevented her from taking the argument further.

Fortunately, they were promised that evening to a levee at Lady Merrivale's—a lady known to Pa and the first of their many invitations—and Alice, self-centered as always, quickly lost interest as more important issues took pride of place, and became wholly preoccupied with what she should wear. Sir Charles, arriving home early, was consulted and, stifling a sigh, declared that she would look divine whatever she wore.

He sounded tired, Cressida thought, but when she ventured to quiz him, he would only vouchsafe that there was much to be decided, a situation made more complex by a disturbing degree of discontent, in some cases verging on dissent, among the representatives of the participating governments. "They resemble nothing so much as a lot of squabbling schoolboys," he declared.

However, he was seldom blue-deviled for long, and by evening all was apparently forgotten, Alice having coaxed him into a more cheerful frame of mind, which, to give Alice her due, could be accounted as one of her few redeeming qualities. So much so, in fact, that Cressida, watching her father later as he laughed and joked with every appearance of a man at ease, supposed that anyone observing him would take him to the life and soul of the party, as if he hadn't a care in the world. But she knew him too well. Had someone been indiscreet about Alice in his hearing?

Lady Merrivale's salon was crowded. Some people Cressida already knew, and her ladyship was eager to make others known to her, including her daughter, Arabella, whom she did not take to, finding her rather too haughty for her liking.

"Such a charming gown you are wearing, my dear," her ladyship gushed. "I can't recall ever having seen that particular colour or style anywhere—such a vibrant pink—and you carry it so well."

"Madame Fanchon, who designed it, referred to it as a Chinese robe," Cressida said. "I confess it is one of my favourites."

But later, as she lay wide awake, Cressida's thoughts returned to her father. Had someone, she wondered, been indiscreet concerning Alice in his hearing? The thought kept her awake long into the night, but she knew she could never bring herself to quiz him on so delicate a subject.

Chapter Eighteen

Time was flying past at a dizzying pace, and scarcely a day went by without at least one invitation being added to the already overcrowded mantelshelf, until Cressida's prediction that they would scarcely be a night at home proved to be nothing less than the truth.

Alice was clearly enjoying every minute. No longer sharp-tongued—she positively glowed with good will. Cressida wasn't sure that she didn't prefer the old Alice, but as she was rarely at home, it scarcely mattered, though at the back of her mind Cressida wondered about the old friends with whom she spent so much time. And, more than once she had heard Alice's name linked with von Schroder. Had Pa heard them, too?

About that, she was less sure. Difficult negotiations were the breath of life to Pa, and she had often heard him declare that the more lively and contentious they became, the more of a challenge they represented. Equally, he was known to enjoy the socializing that went with it, and never tired of the endless discussions. But a few times recently Pa's temper had been on a short rein, which was quite out of character. Cressida wasn't convinced that this was entirely due to the increasingly quarrelsome nature of the delegates. Rather, she suspected that he had heard some of the many rumours concerning Alice and the count. In fact, it would be wonderful if he had not been made aware of it, for Alice was less than discreet, and the two were so often seen together that it was fast becoming one of the most widely discussed on-dits among the many that proliferated.

Cressida wondered how Pa would take rejection if Alice abandoned him for von Schroder. His pride might well be dented, for as a rule it was he who tired of relationships, though she had never known him to be unkind in his dealings with the ladies. On the contrary, he was well known for his generosity, so that almost all of his mistresses remained on good terms with him.

Count von Schroder, on the other hand, lacked even a drop of the milk of human kindness. What he did have was arrogance in full measure, together with a title, a considerable fortune, and a dangerous combination of charm and brutality which some women, it seemed, found irresistible.

One might have thought that Alice, being older, would be blessed with sufficient wisdom and experience to see through him, but as yet she had shown little evidence of it, and would undoubtedly be furious to find her judgement called into question. All she seemed to care about was that he had a title more prestigious than her own, together with a certain brutal charm, an immense fortune and a town house of palatial proportions, as well as a shooting lodge a mile or two out of town. Cressida suspected that she had long since gone through most of her own money, which was probably one of the reasons she had latched on to Pa in Paris.

But Pa, as Alice had discovered to her cost, was no fool in spite of his weakness for a pretty face. He thrived on the cut and thrust of diplomacy, and though generous enough in his casual way, everything else, Alice and even occasionally herself included, came second to aiding Castlereagh in his determination to secure an agreement favourable to all.

Being overlooked was something Alice had not anticipated and her pride was hurt. And so, in her usual impulsive way she had turned to von Schroder, who fed her vanity with fine words, flattered her, and made her feel desirable. Cressida feared that her very eagerness could be her undoing, to say nothing of her stubborn streak. Also, the count thrived on domination—the subjugation of his prey. And, since she suspected that Alice would not be easy to subjugate, she could well be putting herself in extreme danger. If so, Cressida found it increasingly difficult to erase from her mind the fate that had befallen Isabella. It was even more disturbing to discover from a comment innocently let slip by Frau Helger, that Alice had taken to sleeping in the spare bedroom, her excuse being that she did not wish to disturb Sir Charles if she should return very late at night. When questioned further, the housekeeper reluctantly admitted that on more than one occasions, the bed had not been slept in at all.

Cressida wondered if her father knew that the affair had gone so far. If so, he was hardly likely to admit it. Only the certain knowledge that any attempt on her part to take issue with Alice would do more harm than good prevented her from speaking out.

However, with the parades and balls and other entertainments gathering pace, there was much to do and little time to brood, so that she herself was scarcely a night at home. Even so, she could not, as Alice frequently did, spend most of the morning in bed. Instead, she made it her business to be down in time to take breakfast with her father, which seemed to please him.

"This is like old times, what?" he said one morning as she poured him a second cup of coffee. "I'd forgotten how pleasant it could be—just the two of us."

Surprised but pleased, Cressida replied with enthusiasm, "Oddly enough, I had been thinking the very same thing. It is good, isn't it? We are much more comfortable here, of course, though life was never dull in those days, even if we sometimes wondered where we were to lay our heads at night." She laughed. "Do you remember that odd little woman in Salamanca, the time I went with you into Spain? She gave us shelter in that terrible hovel and spoke no English, but she made the most mouth-watering tortillas."

He didn't respond immediately, then, "We've had some fine old times, you and I, haven't we, Cressie?" he said, sounding suddenly weary. This upset Cressida for he was never tired, even at the end of the longest day, although she guessed he was disheartened rather than tired, and suspected that it wasn't solely Congress business that was at the root of his present frame of mind.

She said impulsively, "You know, Pa, you mustn't let Alice's odd behaviour upset you. I'm sure she does not mean to neglect you. It is simply that she is, by nature, a creature of the night, and as such is seldom wide awake much before midday, by which time you are long gone."

He immediately seemed to pull himself together and leaned across to pat her hand, saying ambiguously, "Y're a good girl, Cressie—better and wiser than I deserve, silly old fool that I am, sometimes."

"You are not silly, nor are you old!" she retorted. "And I won't have you say such things. You know perfectly well that this wretched Congress would all but fall apart without you."

"Perhaps." He laid his napkin aside and stood up. He bent down and kissed her cheek. As he reached the door, he said without turning 'round, "Y're a good girl. But, whatever you may think, I'm not blind, y'know." And she realised immediately that he was well aware of Alice's latest flirtation. It was inevitable, of course, for Vienna was a perpetual sea of gossip.

However, Cressida told herself that no good would come of brooding, for life would go on its merry round, come rain or shine. And so she allowed herself to be swept along, quite often in the company of Prince Metlin, until they were in danger of being talked of as a pair, which he took nobly in his stride.

However, it infuriated Alice, who, in spite of having Count von Schroder dancing attendance on her, was bitterly jealous, and unwise enough to voice her feelings when she and Cressida were forced into each other's company at one of the many afternoons where delicious morsels of scandal were exchanged over the teacups.

"I suppose you are aware of the gossip surrounding you and Metlin," she said, taking Cressida aside and scarcely bothering to lower her voice. "I am surprised your father allows the association, for nothing can come of it. The prince is a known flirt, but I doubt he will ever contemplate marriage."

"Well, I must say that is rich coming from you," Cressida retorted, for once failing to hold her tongue. "As it happens, Prince Metlin is a friend from many years back. Pa knows and trusts him implicitly, in the certainty that he would never do anything to harm me, or my reputation." Once released, all the aggravation of the past few weeks poured out of Cressida. "Would that the same could be said of your present liaison. I hope you don't think you are hoodwinking Pa, for he knows—I should think everyone knows—about you and von Schroder. In fact, I wonder you have the gall to remain under our roof, expecting Pa to support you. If you had a spark of decency you would leave—challenge your lover to accept his responsibilities. But perhaps you are not confident that he would do so, for everyone knows von Schroder is not to be trusted."

"How dare you speak so to me," Alice said spitefully. "You are insolent beyond belief."

"Perhaps. But at least I am honest."

For a moment Cressida thought the older woman would strike her. But after glaring at her with a malevolence that quite marred her fine looks, Alice stormed out of the room.

In the days that followed, Cressida took good care to avoid her, though indeed Alice was so often absent, that their paths seldom crossed. And as life grew ever more hectic, and Sir Charles was seldom home, her presence was scarcely missed.

There were balls and banquets, faked tournaments and lots of amateur theatricals and *tableaux vivants*; there were exhilirating sleighing expeditions to the Wienerwald, from which the guests returned in darkness accompanied by mounted footmen carrying flaming torches. And still to come early in November was a grand *redoute paree* which Prince Métternich was to host, and many a *tableaux vivant* as well as ballets and balls by the score. All these pleasures were exhilirating, but there were moments when she craved peace and quiet.

"I perceive you are as weary as I feel, though you do not show it," Prince Metlin murmured one evening, finding Cressida sitting alone in the conservatory of yet another grand duke, listening to the distant music drifting out from the ballroom as it mingled with the gentle splash of a fountain. "In fact," he murmured, putting up his glass to admire her amber silk gown and the matching gold circlet set with amber beads that Jane had threaded into her hair, "I believe I have never seen you look finer."

"You are very kind to say so, Alexei," she said, smiling up at him and thinking him an equally fine figure in his cavalry uniform. "I am not exactly weary. More likely it is a case one ball too many. And perhaps a feeling of guilt. I was in danger of being promised to an extremely dull, boring grand duke for the supper dance, but suddenly I felt unable to face the thought of it, and told him I was already promised. And then I felt guilty and so, craving a few moments of quiet, I slipped away."

He thought she looked enchanting with her lower lip trapped between even white teeth—like a child caught out in some misdemeanor. He chuckled. "Poor duke. Would you prefer that I should also leave you?"

"Oh, no! Please don't go—sit and talk to me for a few minutes for you are never boring. And I shall be myself again directly. Indeed, I must go back, or Pa will wonder where I am."

"There is a time for talk, but this is not it. Instead you will allow me to escort you, for there is someone I particularly wish you to meet." His eyes twinkled as she tried to hide her dismay. "You have a very revealing face, *moya dorogoya*, but I think—indeed I hope—that I may succeed in surprising you—and perhaps please you a little also." He rose and offered her his arm. "Shall we go?"

By now thoroughly intrigued, she allowed herself to be escorted back towards the ballroom where the music was coming to an end—and was just in time to catch a glimpse of her father watching Alice, who, clad in an exquisite white lace gown, was being whirled around by Count von Schroder. Her hair, shining like spun gold, was piled high and threaded through with more white lace, and curiously, she had chosen to add a provocative eye patch of the same lace. But she didn't look as though she was enjoying herself. Cressida's mind raced wildly—could the patch be hiding some disfigurement? Surely the count could not— would not . . . ? But a corner of her mind whispered, "Oh, but he would!"

She turned to her father. Had he also thought the eye patch strange? His features gave nothing away, but then, he had always been adept at hiding his feelings, so that anyone not knowing him well would suppose him to be in high good humour. But it was immediately clear to her that Alice's days were numbered. Cressida ought to have been glad, for she longed for him to find a soul mate, and that Alice could never be. Even so, something about that eye patch troubled her. What was it a mere gesture of eccentricity, or—and here she thought the impossible—could the patch be hiding something—a sore eye, perhaps? Or something more sinister? Oh, surely not!

So wrapped in her thoughts was she that she hardly noticed the music coming to an end. The prince's touch on her arm startled her.

"Come," he said, guiding her with the precision of an expert beyond the reach of the couples who had begun to disperse, moving amid the murmur of conversation in a graceful, colourful tide. Puzzled, but intrigued, she saw that they were approaching a small antechamber where, through the half-open door, she caught a brief glimpse of two elegant gentlemen engaged in a conversation which ceased as they entered. But even before they turned she had recognized them.

"Alastair! Perry! Oh, what a wonderful surprise!" Her heart was thudding against her ribs as she hurried forward, extending a hand to each, quite uncaring of her blushes as each hand was lightly kissed. Alastair retained her hand for much longer than was necessary, treating her to a minute scrutiny, and something in the way he looked made her heart beat even faster. She had once thought his eyes were cold, but now they seemed to glow like sapphires, so deeply blue they were almost black.

As for Alastair—for perhaps the first time in his life he found himself bereft of words upon seeing Cressida in her slender amber gown, her eyes shining with excitement—and—dare he hope—something more. It was as if a part of himself that had long been frozen had suddenly come alive.

"But how—why are you here?"

He wanted to say, "Because London—no, life—itself had lost all its savour once you were gone." Instead he hear himself telling her blandly that her letters to Aunt Beatrice had aroused his interest.

"Quite simply, we were both so intrigued that we decided we must come and experience the reality for ourselves."

"But where are you staying? For we are constantly being told that everywhere is filled to suffocation. There is not a room to be had."

"Ah, therein lies our good fortune," Alastair explained. "For Perry has an ancient and most obliging great uncle who lives on the outskirts of Vienna, and he was so delighted to see his great nephew, even if Perry was looking more than a shade sickly, that he insisted we should stay with him."

"Never could abide ships, y'see," Perry murmured, lifting her hand to his lips and smiling his gentle endearing smile. "However, it was but a small sacrifice, and now that I bask in the warmth of your smile, my dear Cressida, the exigences of the journey are little more than a fading memory."

"A great one for tipping the butter boat is Perry," Alastair murmured. "Never at a loss for the right word."

"But then, he is always the perfect gentleman," she said, determined to maintain a lighthearted approach so that he would not be aware of the confusion within her.

"Whilst I am almost always an imperfect one," he replied urbanely, and had the satisfaction of seeing her lips quiver. "I hope you mean to reward me with a dance?"

All Cressida's fine intentions melted away in an instant as she felt herself blushing. It was quite ridiculous that Alastair should have such an effect upon her, but in truth she had suddenly realized how much she had missed him, and was glaringly, gloriously aware that it was his very presence that made her heart suddenly beat faster. He, like Perry, was at his most elegant in a black swallow-tailed coat and the now fashionable slim trousers, which stood out to advan-

tage amid all the more flamboyantly dressed gentlemen. He might not rival Perry in the exquisite
arrangement of his cravat, but in her eyes he was
perfection.

She realised that Alastair was still awaiting her answer, and endeavoured to compose herself, mustering
a touch of humour as she made a great play of perus-
ing her card. "A dance—yes, indeed—I believe I can
fit you in before supper." She saw his lips quiver, and
hurried on, "In fact, your arrival is quite providential,
for I am being pursued by an egregious little duke
from some obscure principality who insists that I must
honour him with the supper dance which happens to
be a waltz, and not only is the said gentleman a hopeless dancer who once mangled my feet—he is also a
dead bore. I have managed to resist his overtures thus
far, but am finally out of excuses, which is why I took
refuge in the conservatory where Alexei found me and
came to my rescue."

"Oh, fortunate prince," murmured Mr. Devenham.

Cressida could feel herself blushing, but the twinkle
in Alexei's eyes reassured her that he had taken no
offence, and set her at ease.

"The supper dance it shall be, then," Alastair said.
"After all, we cannot allow your digestion to be ruined on such a beautiful evening."

She found herself wishing that the time would pass
more swiftly. But at last the moment arrived. He held
her firmly, whirling her around until the chandeliers
seemed to splinter into shards of light above them,
and reality ceased to exist. His breath caressed her
cheek, his hand was warm and intimate in the small
of her back. Cressida wished that the music would go
on forever.

But like all good things, it came to an end and she
was obliged to relinquish her delightful air-dreaming
and be sensible once more.

"How is Isabella?" she asked during supper. "It is very remiss of me not to have inquired before now."

"She is getting stronger every day," Alastair said. "And although nothing has been said, I am convinced that in a very short time she will marry Harry. They have become very close, and in a curious way are helping to heal one another. To my immense pleasure he has taken the lease on a small farm on Langley land, and means to settle down to enjoy a fruitful life in the country. If all goes well it could be the making of both of them, and, given time, I have it in mind that he might run the estate for me."

And will it also please you to have Isabella so near? she wondered. But aloud she said, "Indeed. I couldn't be more happy for them. Like you, I believe they will be good for one another."

At that moment she looked up, and across the room and saw von Schroder at another table, watching her, with Alice beside him, head bent. The fixed concentration of that look reminded her of a snake she had seen once in Spain, the moment before it struck. She shivered, and for a moment could not look away. Finally his glance moved on to Alastair, with naked hatred in his eyes. Then they came to rest once more upon her. She shivered and turned away to speak to Alastair.

"Now, please, do tell me about Lady Bea," she said, too swiftly. "I have had several letters, of course, but one cannot always tell from letters. Is she as well as she seems?"

Alastair shot her a curious look, but already Cressida had pulled herself together, so after a moment he replied, "I believe so. Missing you, of course, though your letters keep her entertained. And we have been hearing great things of your father which pleases her, I think."

"Yes, indeed. She is very fond of Pa. In fact . . ." Cressida paused, biting her lip. And then, meeting the query in his eyes, blushed. "I daresay you would have been old enough to have heard the rumours at the time—about there being some talk of them marrying . . . But then he met Mama, and it was love at first sight."

"Highly romantic," he murmured.

"But not very kind, I think. Pa has many excellent qualities, and I love him dearly, but I am not blind to his faults." She stopped, bit her lip and realised that having started, she must finish. "So I have to admit that he does not always stop to consider the feelings of others. Which I suspect that was so in the case of Lady Bea. I believe she took it very hard," she continued, blushing.

He shrugged. "I seem to remember there was the usual amount of gossip at the time, though it largely passed me by. And shortly afterward she married Kilbride. I was only a young stripling at the time, and thought little of it."

There was a dryness in his voice that made her blush. She concluded hastily, "Of course not. There was no reason why you should. But all is now forgiven, if not forgotten, and she and Pa are able to meet as friends. As for the present situation, I believe Lord Castlereagh finds my father a great source of calmness and sound common sense amid all the quarrels and confusion."

Alice was not mentioned, though he must surely have seen her, and Cressida had no desire to bring her into the conversation. As for the eye patch, if he had not noticed, it was not for her to bring it to his attention.

It was rather later, when supper was at an end and people around them were drifting away, that she finally felt obliged to broach the subject of Alice, and von Schroder. The wine had loosened her tongue and Cressida found herself confiding in him that her father might be taking Alice's defection hard.

"Their relationship is no longer what it was," she

murmured, under cover of the buzz of conversation surrounding them as people departed. "Pa is busy and tired, and is not getting any younger, whilst she did nothing but complain that she never saw him, and is not used to coming second. But much as I have grown impatient with Alice, I wouldn't wish her to be hurt, and from what we already know of von Schroder. . . ."

"You worry too much," he said abruptly. "Alice is not an innocent like Isabella—I'd say she is well able to take care of herself."

It was a decided rebuff, and she wished with all her heart that she had kept her opinions to herself. After all, Alice had treated him very badly, so he had little reason to sympathise. And, that being the case, she thought it wiser not to mention the curious nature of the eye patch.

She did manage to explain the gist of her worries to Perry later, however. He was kinder than Alastair, but his judgment was not so very different.

"I wouldn't let her trouble you, m'dear girl. Not one to cut up a character, as a rule—but they do say that you reap as you sow. Suffice it to say that Alice has done her fair share of sowing—dashed near ruined Alastair's life in the process. Wouldn't care to think of her being ill-treated, of course, but she seems well able to look out for herself. And your father is a sensible fellow—a trifle oversusceptible to the lure of a pretty face, perhaps—often so with powerful men, I believe—but at the end of the day he's astute enough to discard shoddy goods. In fact, I'd hazard from what you inferred that he's already seen the light. And once that happens, the outcome is inevitable. Best thing all round, I'd say. Sir Charles will come about. He ain't the kind to be brought low for long by a light-minded young woman."

"Why, so I hope," she said with a sigh.

"My word on't, you'll see."

She smiled at him, much cheered by his calm good sense, and knowing in her heart that he was right.

Much later, she had danced the cotillion with her father, and had found him in such good spirits that her worries all but faded away. "Your mother would be proud to see you now," he declared. "I vow there ain't a young lady in the whole room can hold a candle to you!"

She looked around at all the ladies in their finery, and wondered how many of them he had wooed with similar extravagant compliments.

"Dear Pa," she said affectionately. "I fear you are biased, but I love you for thinking it. And you are right," she concluded as the cotillion came to an end. "Mama would be proud—of both of us."

"Y're a good girl," he said, much moved. "Now, we must find your friends."

"Oh, you mustn't worry about me, Pa," she said. "I wish to find Lady Merrivale and have a few words with her before I go back to join the others."

"Well, if you're sure . . ."

"Quite sure," she said. And watched him thread his way through the crowds, stopping to have a word here, and a laugh there. She smiled and turned to seek out her ladyship, only to discover that the count had appeared from nowhere—or so it seemed—to block her path.

"Fraulein Merriton." He was scrupulously polite, but one only had to look into his face, flushed with too much wine, his eyes hard and brilliant, to recognise the danger signals. She suppressed a shudder of apprehension as he continued, "You are an elusive creature—or perhaps you have been deliberately avoiding me."

I must keep a guard on my tongue, she thought. This is no place to come to cuffs. Also, any hint of such behaviour would not reflect well on Papa.

"Not so," she said with cold formality. "On the contrary, I have been so much in demand that I have not had a moment to give you so much as a thought." She saw his mouth tighten. "And now, if you will excuse me, my friends will be wondering where I am."

"Ah, yes, Langley . . . and his tame companion," he almost ground the words out. "I find it most curious that he is here."

The slur implicit in his voice roused her to fury, which led her to exclaim, perhaps unwisely, "You would do well not to underestimate Lord Langley— or indeed Mr. Devenham, who is not quite as indolent as he would appear."

"Even so, they are guests in my country, as indeed you are. As such, it is expected that you are required to show me some respect."

"As you did when you visited England, which is my country? I have seen what you are capable of—and had you not run away in such a cowardly fashion, you would have been called to account for it."

His flushed face darkened with the force of his anger, though his voice was silky soft. "You are insolent, fraulein. Have a care, or you may yet have cause to regret such impetuous language."

"What will you do? Black my eye as I suspect has been Alice's fate? Such a pretty eye patch she is wearing. It quite makes one curious to learn what secrets lie beneath it."

There was a moment of uncanny silence, and looking around Cressida saw that the supper room was now all but empty. She felt suddenly horribly vulnerable and not a little afraid, as too late she realised the folly of allowing her tongue to run away with her.

And then Perry's voice, sounding blessedly normal, broke the silence.

"Ah, here you are, Cressida, m'dear. We had been wondering where you had vanished to. I believe you are promised to me for the quadrille." He turned to the count, his voice politely cool. "You will forgive us, I'm sure—daresay you have a partner waiting for you."

There was an uncomfortable moment when anything might have happened. Then Count von Schroder clicked his heels and gave a brief jerky bow. "Until the next time, Fraulein Merriton. For there will most assuredly be a next time."

His words sent a shiver through her. As he strode away she let out a sigh of relief. "Thank you, dear friend. My situation was in danger of becoming a trifle awkward."

"Quite." Perry paused, then added, "No wish to preach, m'dear, but I beg you will not underestimate that fellow's capacity for evil."

"Oh, I assure you there is no danger of that," she said, almost too quickly. "I know exactly how the count's mind works, and have no intention of falling into any of his traps."

Her apparent confidence for some reason made him more rather than less uneasy, and although he was wise enough not to voice his fears, he resolved to mention his unease to Alastair.

Chapter Nineteen

Cressida slept late, and awoke to find the sun streaming in through a gap in the curtains. A slight sound drew her attention to Jane, who was on the far side of the room, quietly folding away a pile of freshly laundered garments.

She struggled to raise herself on her pillows. "What time is it?"

"It's goin' on ten o'clock, give or take a few minutes."

Cressida was shocked. "But it can't be!" She peered at the little Viennese clock on the mantelshelf. "Heavens!" She pushed back the blankets to swing her legs round. "I never sleep that late!"

"You don't often make a habit of staying out until three o'clock in the morning, neither," Jane said placidly.

"Even so."

"Even so, nothing. There's no call to panic. Just stay where you are. It won't do you any harm for once. I'll just finish this lot, then I'll make you some breakfast. The old biddy's gone out to do her shopping, and Sir Charles has been gone a couple of hours or more since, so you can take your time."

It was totally against her nature to linger in bed, but after a moment's reflection, Cressida capitulated. As Jane closed the door quietly behind her, she lay back against the pillows, shut her eyes, and allowed her mind to drift over the events of the previous evening—the good and the potentially unpleasant. And of these, it was the latter that mostly occupied her thoughts.

Common sense dictated that, braggart and bully though he was, Count von Schroder would not be stupid enough to harm Alice seriously—and, even less would he attempt to wreak his vengeance on herself—not with Pa in a position to expose his villainy to the highest authorities in Vienna, where rumors already abounded. Except that, when his passions were aroused, common sense didn't come into it. And with hindsight she realized that it had been foolish of her to incur the count's wrath.

Her musings came to an abrupt end as the door opened to admit Jane bearing a loaded tray which included a large coffeepot, a milk jug, a dish of fruit, and a large plate of crisp rolls, butter, and honey.

"Goodness, I'll never eat all that!" she exclaimed, as it was set down on the table beside her.

"You never know what you can do till you try. In my opinion, you don't eat enough. Not that you ever heed what I say . . ." The maid paused, and something in her voice made Cressida look at her more closely. "You'd best know, I suppose," she said reluctantly, " 'er ladyship's back. An' from the little I saw of her before she shut the door an' turned the key, she's not lookin' all that bright, to say the least."

Cressida's heart hollowed, as she remembered her misgivings concerning Alice. She swung her legs out of bed. "Pass me my wrap, Jane. I'd better go to her."

"You stay where you are. Later'll be soon enough. There's no call to be lettin' a good breakfast spoil . . ."

"I won't. But I won't enjoy it either until my mind is set at rest."

Cressida knocked on the spare-room door. When nothing happened, she turned the handle, but found it locked. "Alice—please let me in. I know you're there."

There was silence. Then, "Go away," came the muffled reply.

"I will not. Not until I'm satisfied that you're all right." When there was no reply, she rattled the handle noisily. "I mean it, Alice. I'll break the lock if I have to, and don't think I can't, for I've acquired a great variety of skills in my travels." Cressida feared her threats were falling on deaf ears, and was about to turn away when she heard the key turn in the lock. She tried the door again and it swung open.

The older woman had already turned away and was sitting on the end of the bed, with her back to the door, her wrap clutched around her, and her beautiful fair hair dishevelled and falling forward as if to shield her face. Cressida closed the door quietly and walked across to her.

"Alice?" There was no response, and she continued to avert her gaze. "Alice, please listen to me. I know we haven't dealt very well together of late, but I have no wish to see you unhappy—or worse, seriously harmed. And I know only too well that Henri von Schroder can be a vile, unscrupulous man, for I have seen the results of his cruelty."

Still there was no reply. And then, just as she was about to take her by the shoulders, Alice slowly turned toward her and Cressida uttered a stifled gasp, for not only did she have a black eye, a number of bruises, and a cut lip; from the oddly stiff way she was holding herself, it seemed certain that the beating had not stopped there. He must have been enraged, for as with Isabella he had departed from his usual habit of causing hurt where it did not show.

"Oh, Alice!" Cressida crouched down in front of her. "I am *so* sorry!"

"I don't know why you should be," came the muffled reply. "After all, you did try to warn me. But I thought I knew better." She uttered something between a laugh and a moan. "I even, God help me, relished that hint of danger—was so sure I could handle Henri. So the fault is entirely mine."

Her admission was true enough, but this was no time to be attaching blame. "Never mind all that for now. I'll get Jane to put some water on to boil. You'll feel better after a soak in Frau Helger's ancient tub."

To her distress the older woman began to cry—hard painful sobs. It was so out of character that Cressida scarcely knew how to react. Give her a crisis, or a difficult situation to resolve, and she would attack it with enthusiasm and determination. But tears almost always embarrassed her. And to add to her discomfort, in her heart she suspected that she was partly to blame and von Schroder had taken out his fury against herself on poor hapless Alice.

"Oh, Alice, don't—please don't cry!" she said awkwardly. "I have a big pot of salve, and when you've had your soak Jane will apply some, and maybe bring you some coffee, and you'll soon feel more the thing."

"I don't know why you're being so kind to me. I've been such a fool!"

"Perhaps. But I daresay we are all guilty of behaving foolishly at some time in our lives," Cressida said. "Also, I am aware that I haven't exactly made things easy for you. However, let us not apportion blame over what is past. The thing is, we both of us know that in this instance it is the count who is the real villain." She hesitated, then asked diffidently, "Are you badly hurt? If you need a doctor or anything . . ."

"No! Oh, no!" came the too-quick reply. "I shall soon mend. But I would appreciate the coffee . . ."

As tears threatened again, Cressida hurriedly left the room and went in search of Jane, who clearly thought her mistress had taken leave of her senses, though she refrained from actually saying so. In fact, her lips remained clamped tight—an unfailing way she had of demonstrating her disapproval.

"Well, what else could I do?" Cressida exclaimed in an attempt to justify what Jane clearly saw as madness. "She looked so lost and vulnerable, and for the very first time I found myself feeling sorry for her."

"I daresay you did. You was always a soft touch for any wounded creature, an' it's my guess she'll be nursing some tidy bruises for a while. Mind, I'm not sayin' what that count done was right—in fact, he deserves a good thrashin' hisself in my opinion, except his sort almost always get off payin' for what they do. It's to be hoped that 'er ladyship'll be sadder and wiser for the experience—though her kind seldom learn." Her piece said, Jane's voice softened slightly. "Any road, I'll see to that bath an' mebbe take her some coffee later."

Having done all she could, Cressida pushed Alice's fate to the back of her mind. She had recently purchased a new riding habit and had been eager to wear it that afternoon when she was to ride out with Alastair. The dressmaker was no Madame Fanchon, but she was more than competent and wickedly expensive. The habit was fashioned of tan cloth in a military style, with much black braiding on the fitted jacket and the hem of the skirt, and with it she wore black half boots and a neat black hat *à la* Hussar.

"Very fetching," Alastair murmured, one eyebrow lifting and a gleam in his eyes as he tethered his own horse in order to assist her to mount.

"I think so, too," she agreed, her lips quivering with amusement, feeling very strange, like a green girl, when he clasped her ankle to guide her foot into the stirrup, and holding on to it for considerably longer than was necessary.

Later, in the Prater, they met up with Prince Metlin, who eyed them with interest. "Not spoiling sport, am I? I can easily make myself scarce."

"You will do nothing of the kind. I hope you know

you are always welcome," Cressida insisted, a little too readily. In a bid to turn the conversation, she found herself rushing into speech as she told them about Alice.

Alastair swore softly under his breath, but the prince, though sympathetic, advised that she should leave well enough alone. And Alastair agreed. Cressida was surprised and a little disappointed to find them less caring than she had expected.

"The Alices of this world seldom learn from their mistakes," Alastair said abruptly when she took issue with him. "She has already demonstrated that she is no different from the rest."

"I suppose so. But perhaps, after this experience, she may prove to be the exception," she declared, surprised to find herself siding with Alice. "If only you had seen her. She looked—oh, I don't know—defeated. And for the first time, I found myself feeling sorry for her."

Alastair threw her a sardonic glance, one eyebrow raised. "That is very charitable of you, Cressida—surprisingly so, in fact, considering all the complaints you have voiced about her in recent times."

"Perhaps I have. But this was somehow different—and people have been known to change . . ."

"This is true," Prince Metlin said, not unkindly. "And I have no wish to sully the young lady's reputation, but I remember Lady Sherbourne from when she lived here, and in my experience, such people seldom change."

"I couldn't agree more," Alastair said harshly.

"Oh, how can you both be so cynical? I know she treated you badly, Alastair, but surely everyone may be allowed a second chance."

It had been a tactless thing to say. His lips thinned, but before he could utter some cutting retort, they were hailed by Perry, who came up to them riding a rather splendid bay mare. "Beauty, ain't she?" he said, smoothing the graceful neck. "Would you believe it—after all this time, I have just discovered that Uncle Lorenz still keeps a stable some distance from the house, and though he don't ride anymore, he has a pair of beauties besides this lady. Says we're welcome to exercise 'em whenever we please."

"Well, if they're as fine as you say," Alastair declared, "I shall be happy to take him up on the offer. These hired ones leave much to be desired."

The ensuing converation continued to center around horses, and it was as though Alice's plight had never been voiced. Cressida felt indignation rising in her, and was half-inclined to bring it to the fore again—to get Perry's opinion of what had happened. But in view of Alastair's dismissive comments, she decided to wait until she could speak to Perry alone. Her planning proved to be in vain, however, for Alastair preempted her decision by relating to him the morning's events.

"And now, would you believe, Cressida means to forgive all?"

"I didn't say that exactly." She turned to Perry. "But you must surely agree that everyone is allowed a second chance? "

"It is what one would expect of you, m'dear, and as a rule I'm all for being charitable. But in this instance . . ." He looked embarrassed. "I've no wish to cut up a character," he murmured, "but the lady in question has been given many a second chance. Fact is, I fear, that the Alices of this world are mostly survivors—and on the whole seem to find consolation without too much trouble."

"Oh, Perry!" she said, more disappointed than angry. "I never took you for a cynic."

"Nor is he," Alastair murmured. "Like me, he is simply a realist."

Her shoulders sagged a little. "Well, you may all be right. I'm sure Pa is already aware of her goings-on, for I know he no longer feels the same about Alice.

But I hope—in fact, I'm sure that if he turns her off, he will not be ungenerous, which is just as well, for I fear she has already run through most of her own fortune."

"You worry too much," Alastair said brusquely.

"And you don't worry enough," she retorted. "But then, she treated you shockingly badly, so I suppose you have cause to attribute to her the old adage: 'As ye sow, so shall ye reap.' "

She regretted the words the moment they were out. But Alastair's tight-lipped expression convinced her that the most grovelling apology would receive short shift. Even Perry seemed less inclined than usual to take her part, so that she felt like a rebuked child, a feeling that did not sit well with her.

"I'm sorry," she said abruptly, feeling the hot pricking of tears. "Clearly we don't see eye to eye over this. I will relieve you of my company."

"Pray don't go, Cressida." Perry sounded genuinely concerned. But it was Alastair she looked to, and he remained stubbornly silent. "I'm sure we would not have you leave us. And all over a small difference of opinion."

She wheeled her horse, saying over her shoulder, "It is kind of you to make light of it, Perry, but Alastair is probably right. He almost always is."

"Then I will go with you, m'dear."

"Thank you, but I'd be devilish poor company."

"But you will permit me to accompany you as far as the gate?" Prince Metlin pleaded beguilingly. "I am on my way to an assignation—a very beautiful young lady, quite new to Vienna, who wishes to become familiar with its pleasures."

This drew a faint smile from her. "Then she can have no better tutor."

"Damn! Oh, damn!" Alastair muttered, his voice betraying the extent of his wretchedness as he watched her ride away.

"My thoughts entirely, dear old fellow," Perry murmured.

"How could I have been so clumsy?"

Perry said quietly, "Perhaps because you care rather more than you will admit, even to yourself!"

"You know me too well," Alastair said, but the heat had gone out of his voice.

"I thought I did. And if I am right, you will swallow your pride and go after her with all speed."

"And be sent to the right about again. I think not."

Cressida rode home in a mood of the utmost misery and uncertainty. Her father would have to be told, for there could be no hiding Alice's bruises. But as he wasn't likely to return until evening, that decision at least could be deferred.

She arrived to be informed by Jane that her ladyship had gone out some time ago. "Mind, she didn't look fit for it, an' so I told her, but she came over all Friday-faced, an' insisted that she needed some fresh air, an' it weren't for me to tell 'er otherwise."

It seemed, on the face of it, a reasonable enough decision to get some fresh air, except that nothing about Alice's present condition was reasonable—especially at this moment

"I suppose she didn't happen to mention where she was going?"

"No." Jane's lips were tight pursed. "She didn't say nothing more, an' I didn't reckon it were my place to ask all hunched and muffled up as she was."

"I fully understand," Cressida agreed hastily. "It wasn't meant as a criticism." Even so, something about the news troubled her. If nothing else, in the circumstances one would expect Alice to hide herself away.

Cressida went upstairs to change out of her riding habit, paused, and decided to take a look in the spare room. All was much as Alice had left it—the bed unmade, her clothes still in the closet. The scene ought to have been reassuring. But something about the whole business didn't feel right.

She closed the door, and on impulse decided to take a look in her father's room. There the signs of Pa's meticulously tidy nature were everywhere to be seen—except for the big corner chest, where one of the drawers had been left slightly open, and on inspection, showed signs of disturbance, which was odd because Pa invariably kept that particular drawer locked, containing as it did items of a priceless and in some cases potentially dangerous nature, including a fine pair of silver-mounted duelling pistols given to him by a grateful Spanish potentate.

With an odd sinking feeling she moved across to examine the drawer more closely, and was disturbed to find quite noticable scratch marks around the lock. She gave the handle a tug and the drawer slid wide open. Her fear turned momentarily to intense relief as she saw that the pistols were still in their beautifully embellished case. But her relief was short-lived, as her attention was drawn to an empty space beside the pistols—a space usually occupied by a dagger with an exquisitely engraved handle, and a blade honed to a lethal sharpness encased in a cutwork leather sheath— yet another mark of gratitude of which Pa was inordinately proud.

He never carried the dagger, except in situations fraught with danger. So why would he need it now? There was no logical explanation for its disappearance unless, perhaps . . . but that was to think the unthinkable. Her heart began to thud.

Was it possible that Alice might have taken the dagger in order to kill the count? Or—and here she hesitated—to perhaps put an end to her own life? As Cressida turned each equally impossible strategy over and over in her mind, she was vaguely aware of the doorbell pealing and wondered why anyone should wish to call unbidden at such an hour. She hurried downstairs to see Jane admitting a familiar figure.

Surprise halted her momentarily, halfway—and then she was running down the last flight, to stop in front of him.

"Oh, Alastair! I am so very glad to see you!"

"Are you, indeed? Well, you may be less pleased to learn that I have come, my dear girl, to discover what the devil you are about."

She held out her hands. "Oh, never mind that, now. The thing is, I find myself in a terrible dilemma and scarcely know which way to turn. And I know you will probably say that it is my own fault, but indeed it is not . . ." Her voice was becoming unsteady.

He had never seen her in such a state of agitation. Her hands, grasping his own, trembled. His first thought was that something must have happened to her father, but his first priority must be to restore calm. "Come, my dearest, most idiotish love, this isn't like you. I suggest we repair to the salon, and Jane shall bring us some tea."

"W-what did you call me?" she stammered, momentarily diverted.

"My idiotish love, which is most assuredly what you are." He took her firmly by the arm and led her, bemused and unresisting, toward the salon, pausing only to say to the shadowy figure standing guard in the shadowy hall, "Some tea, Jane, if you would be so kind."

"Right away, m'lord," she said with surprising mildness, adding with a sniff, "There's a nice fire, an' happen you can talk some sense into herself, meantime."

"It is my intention to do so," he replied with equal mildness.

Jane departed, pleased to see that her mistress was almost herself again. As for his lordship. A proper man, he was—she couldn't have wished for better. At the door she paused. "An' a drop of brandy wouldn't come amiss, the mornin' she's had."

"An excellent idea," he agreed.

The fire in the salon was already burning merrily, and Alastair found himself half-mesmerized by the way its leaping flames lit up the room, turning Cressida's hair to a vibrant red-gold that he longed to touch. He was obliged to collect his wits in order to say calmly, "Now, I wish you will sit down and tell me exactly what you are about."

There was a pause while Jane came in quietly and set down the tray on the small table nearby. "Just ring if there's anythin' more you need," she said, and departed equally quietly.

As Cressida dispensed the tea, she told Alastair, quietly and succinctly, as much as she knew for sure, as well as what she had good reason to suspect. "It wasn't just the evidence of the beating, bad though it was. Alice is much stronger than Isabella and better able to sustain it. The real damage Alice has suffered is in her mind, and as such it has gone much deeper, eating away at her pride and self-worth. And now that the count has all but destroyed that, she has nothing left."

"Surely you could be imagining some of this," he said, not convinced that the woman she described was the woman he knew Alice to be. "The dagger, for instance. Your father could have removed it for his own protection."

Cressida shook her head. "He has only done so twice to my knowledge, and then only in extreme circumstances. Besides—there are other disturbing factors. If you had seen her, you would understand. I doubt she is capable of taking her own life, but I believe she now hates Henri von Schroder with every fibre of her being—quite enough, in fact, to make some crazy attempt to kill him."

"Then, like him or not, he surely needs to be warned."

"I don't see why." Cressida was incensed. "After all he has done, I, for one, would not lift a finger to help him. But Alice needs to be found before she can attempt to carry out her half-crazed desire for vengeance."

"I thought you disapproved of her."

"And so I do, most of the time. But I cannot stand by and have her risk her life over a vile creature like Count von Schroder."

He shook his head, his eyes crinkling into a smile that made her catch her breath. "What a strange girl you are. Then I suppose I had better find her before she can harm von Schroder—or herself."

"Oh, thank you. And I shall come with you."

"Indeed you will not. That would be dangerous in the extreme!"

"Oh, what nonsense. I have faced danger many times, and by now I know exactly what the count may or may not do. Besides," she added persuasively, "Alice will need someone to comfort her and keep her out of harm's way."

He shook his head and bowed to the inevitable.

Chapter Twenty

The count's impressive residence stood remote behind high walls, surrounded by woodland and backed by the distant Wienerwald, which made brilliant swathes of color in the background. The setting seemed so peaceful, so perfect, that but for the two armed guards on the gate, one would never imagine that anything untoward could happen in such a place. And yet, if Prince Metlin was right, it was built like a fortress in order to keep out unwanted callers.

"It would be politic, I believe, if I were to accompany you," the prince had said, upon coming upon them and hearing of their projected mission. "I have a comfortable closed carriage which may be needed. Also I am known to the guards, so they would find it difficult to refuse us admission." It was agreed, with some reluctance on Alastair's part, though even he could not deny that it made sense.

And so it proved. Cressida didn't know exactly what was said, for she had only a smattering of German. But the presence of Prince Metlin certainly proved to be an asset, as did his mention of Emperor Francis's concern for Lady Sherbourne's welfare, which, he hinted, had been conveyed as a matter of some urgency. The ploy worked. They were instantly admitted to the magnificent hallway, and a servant was sent to inform the count of their mission. The others, however, remained, and continued to eye the visitors with deep suspicion.

"I wish you had not insisted on coming, Cressida," Alastair murmured, tight-lipped as they waited. "This could all turn very nasty."

"And I wish you would not worry about me," she replied. Then seeing his frown deepen, added rather more warmly, "Truly, Alastair, I am not a fool, nor am I being vainglorious, for I have been in worse situations and have come away unscathed. Also, the plain truth is, we don't know what state Alice will be in, and she might need the presence of another woman."

"I appreciate your reasoning," he said, the extent of his anxiety showing in his voice, torn as he was between the logic of Cressida's argument and his need to keep her safe. He looked into her eyes, felt the full force of her implacable determination, and knew that he was beaten. "But do, I beg of you, try not to do or say anything rash. I couldn't bear it if anything were to happen to you, dearest girl, and if we are to get out of this place in one piece, I suspect we shall need every bit of luck and diplomacy we can muster."

"But then, in the matter of diplomacy," the prince murmured softly, "Cressida is probably better versed than either of us, for she has grown up with it."

Before Alastair could say more, the guard returned in a state of great agitation, drawing the other servants to one side and breaking into excitable speech.

Prince Metlin spoke sharply to the guard, and eventually he calmed down sufficiently to speak coherently. From the prince's expression, it was immediately obvious that something fairly dramatic was amiss.

"What is it? What has happened?" Cressida demanded. "It's Alice, isn't it? Something has happened to Alice."

Alastair, who had just about managed to make sense of it all, looked up, his face giving little away as he laid a finger across his lips. When at last the man fell silent, she looked from one to the other.

"Well?" she demanded once more.

"There has been some kind of accident," Prince Metlin said, looking rather more serious than Cressida had ever seen him. "A doctor is being sent for, but I have demanded that we be allowed to see von Schroder—and her ladyship—at once."

"And?" Alastiar's voice had a rough edge.

"It is agreed."

This brought a deep universal sigh of relief.

The ornate staircase seemed to wind upward forever, but at last they came to a wide landing, and a little way along Cressida saw a shaft of light signifying an open door. As they approached, the unnerving silence was broken occasionally by an even more unnerving kind of keening, as if of a wounded animal.

Cressida found her heart beating unnaturally fast, for she was suddenly fearful of what they might find beyond that door, and was grateful when Alastair put out a hand to draw her close. "It might be wiser if you waited until . . ." he began softly.

"No, no! I must see for myself . . ." Her voice firmed. "You need not worry about me. I am perfectly all right. It is simply that not knowing is worse than knowing . . . the imagination plays such tricks . . ."

He sighed and gave in, though his hand beneath her arm remained to support her and she found it oddly comforting.

Inside the room there were clear signs of a struggle. But to their astonishment it was the count who lay like a wounded animal across the huge four-poster bed, facedown, his legs drawn up and his fur-trimmed dressing robe awry and splattered with blood. It was immediately clear that the terrible moans came from him, and that he was in agony. But at least he is alive, was Cressida's immediate thought.

"I am the last person he will want near him," she murmured, having satisfied herself that he was still alive. "And besides, Alice will need me more." Alastair was not happy about her decision, but agreed it was probably the better of two options.

Alice was sitting bolt upright and almost unnaturally still in a chair at the far end of the room near the fireplace, her face devoid of expression. One hand rested limply in the bloodstained lap of her white gown, the other hung at her side, clutching Sir Charles's dagger, from which the occasional drip of blood seeped into the carpet.

"Oh, dear God! Alice, what have you done?" Cressida whispered, crouching beside her. There was no sign of recognition. "Alice?"

The older woman stared ahead as though she neither saw nor heard anything or anyone. However, she allowed Cressida to remove the dagger from her clasp and set it on the floor out of reach. Prince Metlin and Alastair, having registered the extent of von Schroder's injuries, were busy questioning the servants, trying to make sense of what had happened. But, whether from fear or a desire to protect their master, they remained stubbornly silent. Only with the arrival of the doctor did any kind of reality return to the scene.

His examination did not take long. He spoke some English and pronounced that the count's injury was not life-threatening, but—and there the presence of Cressida, who had slipped across to join them, caused him to pause, as if seeking a delicate way to describe its full extent and possible consequences.

"Tell the good doctor that he may be quite frank," she murmured to Alexei. "I speak little German, and understand even less, but it does not take a genius to deduce the nature of the count's misfortune. And much as I detest him, I would not wish that kind of injury upon any man. We can only hope that it does not prove fatal."

The prince threw her a wry look. "You are more generous than he deserves, Cressida."

"Not really." She frowned. "For if I am completely

honest, there is a part of me—a very small unworthy part—that longs for him to suffer as he has made so many women suffer."

"One cannot blame you for that. There are many who would be less honest."

"Perhaps," she said wryly. "But, in spite of what I have said, and somewhat to my surprise, it gives me no pleasure to see him so painfully diminished."

The doctor had by now finished his examination, and was crossing the room to examine Alice, who had not moved since they entered the room. Cressida made her excuses to Alexei and followed the doctor, who was clearly perplexed by Alice's lack of response.

"A tragic situation," he murmured in his fractured English, having tried a number of tests. "It is as if she is entirely withdrawn from reality."

"I am not surprised," Cressida said with her usual frankness. And gave him a brief account of her knowledge of the count and his capacity for inflicting pain. "She has been foolish, to be sure, in ignoring that fatal flaw in the count's nature, for I have warned her more than once. Even so, no one deserves to be used as she and others have been by him. It is small wonder that her control has finally snapped."

"Indeed." He seemed impressed by her cool unembarrassed assessment of the situation and of Count von Schroder's character, which was not unknown to him, though it would obviously be unwise for him to admit as much.

"Is he very badly injured?" Cressida asked.

He looked a trifle embarrassed. "He will live, I believe. More than that is for time and the good God to say, my dear young lady."

"And Alice?"

He shrugged. "That also is not for me to determine. Her injuries are painful, but not, I think, of a dangerous nature, and will heal with time. More worrying is her mental state. And I am not qualified to say when or indeed if that will change."

"Oh, how sad."

"Quite so. But for the present I have been entreated by Prince Metlin to seek out a convent willing to take her in—at his expense. And we must wait and hope."

"How like the prince to be so generous!"

"Indeed!" The doctor's voice was dry. "But then the prince's generosity is well-known." He bowed. "And now, if you will forgive me, fraulein, I must go."

"Yes, of course. And thank you," she said. "You have been most kind."

It was a rather subdued party that made its way back to the city. But it was difficult to remain totally miserable for long as the pull of Vienna's vitality inevitably tugged at the spirits. Word of recent events had not as yet reached the masses, and Cressida wished matters would remain so, though she could not banish the image of poor Alice as she had seen her on that afternoon. And of course Pa would have to be told before word leaked out from other sources. She had not looked forward to enlightening him. And rightly so, for he took it harder even than she had expected, blaming himself for neglecting Alice and becoming impatient with her, thus driving her into von Schroder's arms.

"You must not say such things," she reproached him, coming to sit on the arm of his chair. "Alice is anything but naive. I am exceedingly sorry for her, but she is very far from being an innocent. In fact, she used you very ill, for she knew exactly what she was doing, and cared little that she was cuckolding you. She also knew what the count was capable of, for I had warned her more than once, but she chose to ignore his excesses until it was too late."

"Even so." He sighed. "Poor Alice. And from all accounts, I cannot even call the scoundrel to book."

"Oh, Pa!" Cressida put her arms around him. "You

mustn't blame yourself. Truly, you mustn't. Even if it were possible, she is not worth it. Sorry as I am for her, Alice is and always was ambitious and selfish to the core. Did you know that she almost ruined Alastair's life when he was young and vulnerable?" She felt herself blushing. "Only lately, I think, has he come to realize what a lucky escape he had. Apparently, she has always taken what she wanted—only this time she allowed vanity and greed to blind her to the count's true character. And has paid a terrible price."

"Even so, if I had been more caring—had not neglected her—perhaps things might have been different, so I must bear some of the blame." He saw she was about to argue and shook his head. "Don't deny it, my dear. You know my nature well enough—almost broke y'r godmother's heart when she was a gel. But you'll know that, too, I daresay. Oh, I always mean well, but I am totally self-centered and ambitious—always have been . . . your mama was well aware of it, but, God bless her, she loved me just the same."

"Don't! I won't listen to you!" Cressida couldn't bear to see him so brought down. She felt painful tears tearing at her throat. "We are none of us perfect. Mama loved you for all the good traits in your character, which are many, and forgave you the rest. Alice cannot possibly be compared to her, for she is incapable of that kind of constancy. You treated Alice with great generosity, but like a pretty butterfly, she has always been incapable of appreciating that generosity." She sighed. "The most important thing, the only thing now, is that she should be well looked after. And like the kind man that he is, Prince Metlin has elected to arrange everything."

"Good God, no!" Her father looked shocked. "That I cannot allow. Any expense must fall to me. I insist. Whatever she has done, I am, and will continue to remain responsible for Alice . . ."

Cressida swallowed her exasperation. "Well, you

and Alexei must argue that out between you. All that concerns me is that Alice should be safe and in good hands. And if in time she recovers, perhaps she will be a better and wiser person, though I doubt it."

"And what will become of the count?"

"Who knows?" she shrugged. "His condition is not good, but sorry as I am for him, I am even more sorry for the many young women whose lives he has ruined without a thought, and pray that he will never be in a position to do so in the future."

She said something similar to Alastair later that evening when they cried off from yet another ball and were sitting quietly on the sofa in the parlor. "Does that sound very hard?"

He drew her close. "My dearest girl, it doesn't sound hard at all. In fact, I couldn't agree more. If anything, I would say you are more generous than he deserves."

"Not generous. Never that! I simply wish him to be kept where he can never again do any harm." They sat in silence for a few minutes. Then, "Do you know what I would like most of all?" she said dreamily, gazing into the flickering flames of the fire.

"No." His arms tightened about her. "But if you will only tell me, you shall have it."

She chuckled softly. "That is a very dangerous statement to make to a young lady."

"That depends on the young lady."

"The thing I would like most is to go home," she said. "Vienna is very beautiful and I have enjoyed myself enormously, but one can have a surfeit of gaiety and balls. Perhaps it is a failing in me, but I am beginning to find it all rather shallow."

"If you wish to leave, then it shall be arranged," he murmured, bending his head to kiss her long and deeply.

"Oh, but you have hardly been here more than a

week or two," she gasped, emerging pink and dishevelled. "I would not wish to spoil your visit . . ."

"My dear foolish girl, as if you could. Why do you think I came?"

Her heart was beginning to beat rather fast. "You told me why—Lady Bea read my letters to you, and you wished to see all the festivities for yourself."

"I lied," he said, straight-faced.

"Oh!"

"I came, dear Cressida, because my life had become unbearably dull without you. I had no one to come to cuffs with, to make me laugh, to make my heart beat faster whenever she was near . . . in short, I was in mortal danger of falling into a decline . . ."

"Oh, Alastair, do stop!" she cried, between laughter and tears. "You in a decline! You cannot possibly . . . that is, you have never given me the least inkling . . ."

"Never?"

She could feel her cheeks turning pink. "Well, perhaps once or twice I thought, dared to hope, even . . . when we weren't at odds. And then—the thought of your coming all this way . . ."

"I had no choice. I daren't take the risk of you meeting some handsome whippersnapper—with good cause, for you are obviously much in demand. And I've seen the way Metlin watches you sometimes . . ."

"Alexei?" Her laughter pealed out. "Oh, no. He is a good and dear friend, and I am very fond of him, but as for constancy—he is like a butterfly flitting from flower to flower."

He eyed her quizzically. "If you say so. Will your father stay on here? The business with Alice must have hit him hard."

"I doubt it," she said, her head against his shoulder. "Enduring passion was never in his nature—except for Mama, of course. Though, even then . . . but he never knowingly hurt her. Oh, he is upset about Alice, of course. And blames himself. But he is much needed here. There is so much squabbling among the various delegates that he sometimes comes close to despair."

"And what of the rumors that Bonaparte has left Elba and is returning to France?"

"You have heard about that?" Pa will be furious, she thought. "I fear it is true. Pa had hoped to keep the news from leaking out, but already it is causing all kinds of pessimism and panic among the less sensible delegates and many months of work are undone."

"Then the sooner we return home, the better, before any real trouble breaks out. Your father will probably be happier to have you out of harm's way, and I certainly have no wish to see my 'soon to be wife' caught up in fresh conflict."

Her mind was in a whirl—her heart leapt in her breast.

"Is that truly what I am to be? You have never actually said . . ."

He spent an agreeable few minutes assuring her that her fate was sealed, from which she emerged once more breathless and so full of delight that it took a little time for her to come to her senses again.

"But what of Perry? Will he wish to leave?"

"Oh, you know Perry. He'll be happy enough to go along with whatever we decide. Unless he feels obliged to stay a little longer with his uncle, though the old fellow is not exactly enlivening company. It is for Perry to decide."

Chapter Twenty-one

Lady Kilbride was sitting in her front parlour, contemplating the notion of summoning her carriage and going for a drive in the park, the afternoon being sunny, when she heard the doorbell ring, followed by Martha's slow footsteps and her "All right, 'old yer horses. I'm comin' as fast as I can." And then, "Oh, my heavens!" she exclaimed. "Well, would you believe it . . . an' not a word . . ." Other voices joined in and a moment later, the parlour door opened and Cressida came running to embrace her godmother, and close behind came Alastair looking like the cat that got the cream.

"My dears!" Lady Kilbride struggled to her feet, and was immediately enveloped in her godchild's outstretched arms. "Oh, how perfectly splendid!" she exclaimed. "And such a surprise!"

It took some moments before any kind of order could be restored, during which Martha left the room saying she'd arrange for tea to be brought.

"But I don't understand," her ladyship said at last, puffing a little from her exertions. "How are you here? I had thought you still in Vienna."

"We were beginning to tire of the endless round of balls and routs, Aunt Bea," Alastair said, taking her hands and lightly kissing them. "And so, with the possibility of trouble brewing, we decided to come home."

"Of course. How sensible. I'm very glad you did,

for there are all kinds of horrid rumours circulating throughout London that there is to be another war. Do sit down, both of you. You must be quite worn out after so much travelling. Is Perry with you?"

"He is home, but was feeling a little unwell, after the journey."

"And your father?"

"Is remaining in Vienna for the present. There is much still to be done, but it is almost certain that with Bonaparte on the loose once more, the Congress will have to be suspended for the time being."

"Well, I am vastly relieved to see you both safe and sound. Is there any truth in this rumour of war being renewed, do you suppose, Alastair?"

"I haven't as yet caught up with the news. In fact we know little more than you do, if as much, since we have been so long at sea. But it seems very likely according to what I could glean from Sir Charles before we left Vienna."

"Well, Charles will know, if anyone does, and if it is true, I think it very careless of whoever was responsible for keeping that creature safe."

She turned back and was in time to see them exchanging amused glances, and in a blinding flash it struck her that something about them was different. Alastair, in particular, was looking positively benevolent. Were they—could it be? Her heart began to beat quite fast. Oh, if only it should prove to be so!

At that moment cook staggered in with the laden tray and set it down on the table.

Cressida was already on her feet. "Thank you, cook. That looks lovely. You must have worked very hard."

"Well, they say woman's work is never done, miss. But I'm right glad to see you home safe an' sound, just the same. There's no place like home, I say, even if it is a lot busier these days, what with folk comin' an' goin'."

"That will do, cook," Lady Beatrice said.

"Right, m'lady." She bobbed a curtsy and left the room.

Cressida laughed. "She doesn't change, does she, ma'am. Whereas I am delighted to see that you are quite changed. Positively blooming, in fact. I also note that Madame Fanchon is serving you well."

"Do you think so?" Lady Kilbride smoothed the skirt of her very becoming bronze taffety gown and patted her hair. "Madame is certainly most accomodating, to be sure. But never mind about me, for I am longing to know all—what of you two? You are looking positively radiant, Cressida, in spite of your long journey. In fact"—her ladyship paused, putting a hand to her bosom—"if I read you right, I feel almost certain that I may be permitted to wish you well."

"Is it so obvious?" Alastair said dryly. "And we thought we were behaving with exceeding moderation."

"Then it is true!" She clapped her hands. "Oh, this is famous news! I could not be more happy!" She embraced each of them in turn. "A wedding—what fun!"

And what a wedding it was, Alastair's idea of a quiet affair banished by his aunt who was outraged at the thought of her only godchild being married in some skimble-scamble fashion and so it came about that several weeks later, when Sir Charles had returned from Vienna for consultations with Lord Castlereagh, a small but select wedding party assembled to see the happy pair married. Celia Arlington, who was herself to be married later in the year, acquitted herself charmingly in the role of bridesmaid, wearing a pretty pale pink dress, with a matching circlet of flowers adorning her head. She betrayed only the slightest hint of nerves, whilst Perry, at his most elegant, supported Alastair.

"My dear Tilly, doesn't Cressida look quite beauti-

ful!" sighed Lady Kilbride, dabbing away a tear as she
beheld her godchild walking up the aisle on her father's arm, wearing a gown of stiff ivory silk trimmed
with cream lace, closed high at the neck with a row
of tiny pearl buttons.

"Indeed, yes. If my Celia looks half as well when
her time comes, I shall be very delighted."

"Oh, she will I am sure," Lady Kilbride said, a little
too emphatically, for she was sure that no one could
equal Cressida, though privately she herself would
have wished for a longer train, a more ornate head-
dress. But in the end she was more than happy with
the pretty lace cap that adorned Cressida's burnished
hair. And Alastair was every inch the bridegroom in a
black coat and dove grey pantaloons, his lace-trimmed
cravat a miracle of complexity.

"Well, Bea, they make a good pair, don't y'think?"
Sir Charles observed jovially, as he escorted her to
the reception which was to be at Langley House.
"You'll be well pleased, I daresay."

"Oh, yes, indeed." She dabbed away a tear with a
scrap of lace. "Very fine. Indeed, I couldn't be
happier."

"The match would have pleased Arabella, too,
don't y'think?"

And Lady Kilbride was able to answer for once
without that little stab of painful memory. "Oh, it
would," she said softly. "In fact, if you will not think
it fanciful in me, I would like to think that perhaps
she knows." Her ladyship hesitated, aware that this
was probably not the right moment to speak. Even so,
the words spilled out. "Charles, I would like you to
know that I am sorry for your recent troubles. That
poor woman once caused Alastair so much grief, you
know, but . . ." He was silent for so long that she
feared she had offended him. "Forgive me," she said
hurriedly. "This is neither the time or the place . . ."

He turned to her with a wry smile. "Y're a good

generous hearted woman, Bea. There aren't many who would be so understanding, and I don't deserve it, for I treated you very badly all those years ago, and nothing much changes. Not very good at being faithful, y'see."

"Arabella didn't think you fickle," she said softly.

"A woman in a million, was Arabella. Put up with my occasional laspes when most would have left me." His looked across the room to see his daughter and new son-in-law in conversation with Perry. Even at a distance their love shone out. "Cressida takes after her mother, thank God. And she has a good man there."

"Why, so I believe," Lady Bea said with pride. "Alastair has been like a son to me, and as for Cressida"—her voice faltered momentarily—"my heart is too full to express all that I owe to her. They have both assured me that as they will only be living round the corner, as it were, so they will be popping 'round quite often."

Alastair had hoped for a moderately restrained reception, but somehow the numbers had grown. Henri Baptiste had excelled himself in preparing a banquet fit for royalty and a wedding cake that Cressida declared much too beautiful to eat.

She was delighted to see that Harry and Isabella were present. They were to be married later that month.

"I need not ask if you are happy," she told them. "It shines out of you like a beacon. And as for you, Isabella—you look so fine and healthy, one finds it hard to remember how ill you were."

"And m-much of her recovery is due to you and his lordship," Harry said. "I shall never forget how caring you were."

"Oh, nonsense," Cressida said. "I am a great believer in Fate—and it is quite plain to me that you are made for each other."

"As are you and his lordship," Harry said. "W-we wish you very happy."

"Thank you. I daresay we may meet frequently, for I am resolved that we shall be using the manor more often in the future."

It was considerably later than they had intended when Alastair and Cressida came to make their good-byes. And they might not have done so then had Alastair not become quite ruthless in his determination to have Cressida to himself. Even so, they had to endure her ladyship's copious tears of happiness.

But at last the happy pair went to change their clothes, whilst Perry had Henry bring the travelling coach to the door, loaded with a veritable mountain of luggage and after many last minute hugs and more tears, and Perry's murmured, "Be happy, my dears," they were away, with Manuel bringing up the rear, riding Vitoria and leading his lordship's fine chestnut mare.

"You haven't told me yet where we are going," Cressida said, her head still in a whirl.

"No."

"Well?"

"It is to be a surprise," he said. "Bonaparte has forced me to change my plans, but I hope you will not be disappointed."

"Oh, Alastair! I wouldn't care if we ended up in some horrid little hovel, as long as we are together."

"Well, I hope I can promise you something rather better than a hovel."

In spite of her avowal that she was not in the least tired, Cressida found her eyes closing more than once, her head drifting towards Alastair's shoulder, until, as the sun sank in a huge red ball, setting the sky alight, she might well have fallen asleep, except that she was suddenly brought to life again as the carriage began to slow down as it approached an imposing pair of gates which were flung open at their coming. And she was suddenly wide-awake again.

"Goodness, where are we?" she asked, straightening up as the carriage turned in and swept up a long curving drive until a final curve revealed a familiar, gracious house built on classical lines.

"Oh, my!" she said softly.

He laughed softly. "Welcome once more, my love, to Langley Manor."

"But I thought . . . that is, I received the distinct impression that you had little feeling for the manor."

"And you, as I recall, took to it the moment you saw it. So I discussed it with Harry and he has been supervising a mammoth overhaul of the place. He's worked like a Trojan, mostly on the inside so far, to make it a place fit for my bride." Alastair drew her close. "I dimly recall that it was once a happy house—when I was small. And I thought, under your influence, it might be so again—a place fit for our children to live in and play in."

She chuckled. "You seem very sure we shall have children."

"Oh, indeed we shall." He bent to kiss her—a long lingering kiss from which she emerged pink and breathless. "In fact, my love, I am impatient for us to begin."